MAKE ME BELIEVE

JILTED: THE BRIDE

TARINA DEATON

TARINA DEATON LLC

ALSO BY TARINA DEATON

The Combat Hearts Series

Stitched Up Heart

Half-Broke Heart

Locked-Down Heart

Rescued Heart

Imperfect Heart

Holiday Heart (only available to newsletter subscribers)

The Jilted Duet

Make Me Believe

Believe In Me (coming Fall 2019)

Susan Stoker World Novel (coming July 2019)

CHAPTER 1

"Are you nervous?"

Rowan glanced at Michael out of the corner of her eye and whispered, "A little. Mostly I'm wondering why I let my sister pick such a long reading."

His lips twitched. "You look beautiful, by the way. I didn't get a chance to tell you before the minister started."

She smiled and looked at him fully. Michael was a true gentleman—always making sure she was comfortable, that she knew he appreciated her, and that she was happy. He was perfect.

Any jitters she had were a perfectly appropriate response to getting married. Promising to love only one person for the rest of her life was a big step.

"You look really good in your tux," she said with a wink.

The custom-tailored tuxedo fit him perfectly. Clean shaven with a fresh haircut, he looked like he'd stepped off the pages of *GQ* or was auditioning to be the next James Bond.

He winked back and turned to face the minister again. Rowan glanced down at her wedding bouquet, softly blew out a breath, and gave her attention to the minister as her sister, Adalynn, finally finished her reading.

The minister glanced between them. In a low voice, he asked, "Are you ready?"

"Yes," they both said.

He raised his voice so the congregation could hear him. "Michael and Rowan, marriage is a promise between two people to love, trust, and honor each other. It takes trust to know in your hearts you only want the best for each other. It takes—"

A commotion at the back of the chapel stopped the minister from telling them what else it took.

"Sir, you can't go in. There's a wedding in progress!"

She recognized their wedding planner Stephanie's voice.

"I know. I'm here to stop it."

Rowan's heart thumped in her chest and her fingers tingled from the flow of adrenaline suddenly coursing through her. She squeezed her eyes closed.

"Please god, no," she whispered. Maybe if she wished hard enough what she thought was about to happen wouldn't.

The strum of a guitar and Luke Stone's smooth, deep baritone filled the chapel.

I hate to interrupt
But do you believe in second chances?
I'm hopelessly romantic
It's true

Our history is rough
But I think I learned some lessons
So this is my confession
To you

Rowan finally glanced to her right. Luke stood tall, proud, and unashamed in the center of the aisle, his gaze directly on her, while he sang. Several guests had their cell phones aimed at him and were likely either recording or streaming live. She couldn't blame them—how often did you get what was essentially a private concert from a chart-topping country singer?

"Rowan." Michael's soft voice pulled her attention away from the train wreck happening in the center aisle.

She saw it in his eyes. The gentleness. The apology. The knowledge that what he did or said next was going to cause her pain, but he was going to do it anyway.

"No," she whispered. He wouldn't. He wouldn't leave her up here alone. He wouldn't walk away from her...from them. Why?

Her head jerked from side to side and she took a jolting step closer. "Don't do this to me."

He shook his head gently. "I'm not doing it to you. I'm doing it for you."

"Michael, please. I love you." The bouquet slipped from her fingers and she reached for his hand.

He grasped hers and squeezed. "I know you do, but you're not in love with me the way you are with him. I've always known that. I love you enough to let you find your happiness, even if it's not with me."

He kissed her cheek and his lips lingered next to her temple. "If you can walk away from him, walk toward me."

She gripped his hand tightly, trying to hold him in place. With a glance at Luke, he turned around and walked away.

CHAPTER 2

Six Weeks Ago

A scream echoed through the building and Rowan jumped. Thankfully, she didn't have the scaler against Mrs. Sherman's gums. She glanced out the door of the exam room in time to see one of the dental technicians, Sierra, jumping excitedly down the hall.

Rowan set her tools on the metal tray next to her and pulled the paper mask away from her face. "Would you excuse me, Mrs. Sherman?"

"Of course." Leaning to the side, she craned her neck as if she could see down the hall. "Maybe her boyfriend finally proposed."

Rowan smiled, swung the dental tray out of the way, and pulled off her gloves. "I think her scream would've been a lot shriller if that had happened."

"Well, hurry back and tell me why she's so excited."

"Will do." Leaving the exam room, she turned left and followed the sounds of excited chatter to the small break room.

Sierra was still bouncing up and down, clutching her phone,

except now Lisa, the office's dental assistant, was jumping with her.

"Y'all! What is goin' on?" She had to raise her voice to be heard over their excitement and her southern accent slipped out a little. She worked hard not to shorten her words or drawl anymore—a habit she picked up in dental hygienist school when she got tired of people assuming that because she spoke slow meant she was slow.

"Justice got floor seats to the Luke Stone concert!" Sierra raised her arms and squealed. "Tenth row center!"

"Wow." Rowan worked hard to put some excitement into her voice. "I thought it was a sold-out show."

"It is, but the radio station is running a contest all month. Justice has been calling in every day trying to win tickets. And he got through today! The best part is we get backstage passes!" She high-stepped in place like a receiver who'd just scored a fifty-yard touchdown and squealed again. "I'm going to get to meet Luke freaking Stone!"

She didn't notice Rowan's half-hearted smile.

Luke freaking Stone indeed.

"WHO NAMES THEIR KID JUSTICE?" her best friend asked.

Rowan propped the cordless phone between her cheek and shoulder, shoved the cork back in the wine bottle, and replaced it in the fridge.

"Colorado hippies. You've lived here long enough you should know that by now."

"Did you get tickets?" Claudia asked.

"VIP, just like always," she said. Rowan's best friend from college understood more than anyone why the tickets were an issue. They'd ended up as roommates when Rowan had transferred to the University of Colorado from Tennessee State.

"Are you going to go?"

"Do I ever?" She carried her wineglass into the living room and curled up in her favorite overstuffed chair.

"There's a first time for everything," Claudia said.

"Not this. I can't. I just—I can't be happy for him and I can't pretend to be."

They had this conversation in some form or fashion whenever his name came up. Ever since the night she'd gotten drunk and tearfully confessed that Luke had chosen being a single, eligible country singer over being the man she'd planned on spending the rest of her life with.

"Besides, what's the point? I'm going to show up with Michael and introduce him to my ex-boyfriend? I can just imagine how that little party would go."

"I know, but they're Luke Stone tickets. I know I'm supposed to hate him, but he is a really good singer and his concerts are supposed to be awesome. Maybe you could go and not go backstage."

She could hear the hope in Claudia's voice. "Claudia, I don't want you to hate him. I don't even hate him and I have plenty of reason to. If you want the tickets, I'll give you the tickets."

"Seriously? You'd do that?"

"Just because I don't want to go doesn't mean you shouldn't go."

"Aren't you going to donate them again?"

"I've been having a hard time finding a charity to take them. Make-A-Wish surprisingly doesn't have anyone that has asked for them this year. There is one charity that might want them to auction off, but they haven't gotten back to me yet."

"Well, damn. I can't take tickets away from a charity. Maybe you should shred them or burn them. It could be cathartic. We'll have a party…light a fire…drink some wine. It can be a thing."

Rowan laughed. "I thought about it the first couple of times, but you're right—he is a good singer and those tickets are hard to come by. Someone might as well get some use out of them."

"Has he tried to contact you? Other than the tickets?"

"No, just the tickets. No notes. No emails. No nothing."

"Maybe he wants you to go to the concert so he can talk to you?"

"And say what? Sorry I was an ass? What good would it do?"

"Don't you wonder what he would say?" Claudia asked.

"No." Lie. "Yes, but what's the point? I love Michael. We're getting married in six weeks. Nothing good will come from me reaching out to my ex-boyfriend."

"You're not even a little bit curious?" Claudia asked.

Rowan sipped her wine, then watched the light amber liquid swirl in the glass. "I am, but I'm afraid of what I'd lose if I went and actually spoke to him. He's my kryptonite and there's a small part of me that will always wonder *what if*. But if I give in to that small part, it would destroy everything I've built with Michael over the last year and a half. I may never love him the way I loved Luke, but that's probably to be expected. I loved Luke the way a girl loves a boy. Michael is kind and wonderful and we love each other the way a man and a woman love each other. I'm not going to jeopardize that to satisfy a little curiosity."

"Rowan, I'm so sorry. I didn't realize it was still so hard for you. I never would have pushed if I'd known."

"It's not that it's hard—it's more like keeping my sweet tooth in check. I'd like nothing more than a bite of double chocolate ganache cake, but I know I won't be satisfied with one bite and I'll eat the whole cake and then I'll have nothing to show for it except a sugar high, a belly full of regret, and ten extra pounds. Best to not even be tempted."

Claudia laughed at her analogy. "Alright. No more chocolate cake."

"Double chocolate ganache cake," Rowan said. "You know

what, you should go. Take Maria. Isn't her birthday coming up soon?"

"She would die. She loves him. Well, she loves his singing. Although if she were straight, she'd probably love him, too."

"Her and fifty million other women," Rowan said. "You can have the tickets on one condition."

"What's that?"

She smiled. She could picture Claudia's look of suspicion. "You have to go dress shopping with me this weekend."

"Please. Like that's a condition. When and where?"

"You didn't let me finish. Adalynn and my mom are coming."

"They're flying out from Tennessee to go dress shopping?" Claudia's voice rose to the point of being shrill.

"Yup. Mom convinced Dad to buy them tickets. In her own words, 'How often am I going to get to help my baby pick out a wedding dress?' "

"Isn't Adalynn on her second marriage?"

"Mom has a selective memory. Plus, Adalynn didn't wear a wedding dress the second time, what with the justice of the peace ceremony and all."

"I'm not really sure I'm getting the better end of this deal," Claudia said.

"True, but I need you on my side. Otherwise my mom and sister are going to have me in some lacy, ruffled monstrosity. With bows and a hoop skirt."

Claudia grumbled low. "They'd better be really good tickets."

"Front row, center."

CHAPTER 3

*L*uke closed his eyes and rested his head back on the couch. He had about thirty minutes before sound check and needed the time to decompress before he had to put on his stage face. The tail end of his first headlining tour was dragging on. He loved it, but he was tired of living out of a bus. Tired of always being on.

His fingers moved randomly over the frets as he strummed. This was when he did his best song writing. No stress to pump out chart-topping songs. Just him, his guitar, and some peace and quiet.

"Do you believe in second chances?"

More and more lately he'd been thinking about a do-over. Wondering what his life would be like if he'd kept going straight instead of taking a hard right. He might be playing professional baseball. Maybe still playing in dive-bars and honky-tonks on the weekends with his college buddies, but at least he'd still be having fun.

When had it stopped being fun? Almost every single one of his dreams had come true—more than he'd ever dared hope for—and all he wanted was to be able to walk into the Piggly Wiggly back home without getting mobbed and the police responding for crowd control.

A melody for a song began to form in his mind. He stopped playing and grabbed his phone, opening the recording app and propping it on the pillow next to him. He hummed a few bars while he played, then the words came.

I let us both down a time or two.
I'd give up everything for you.
What you need to understand
Is I should be your man.
Let's give us a chance again.
Hmmm hmm hmmm hm hm hm...

"I like it. Girls go crazy for a good apology song."

Luke stopped mid-strum and rested his palm over the strings.

Brett, his manager, opened the small fridge in the narrow aisle of the tour bus and grabbed an energy drink. He popped open the can and chugged what must have been most of it before releasing a huge belch.

Luke swiped a hand over his face. He hadn't heard Brett come onto the bus. Even when he was alone, he was never really alone. Constantly surrounded by people, yet he still didn't have anyone he trusted one-hundred-percent. Not even his long-time manager.

"The label wants you back in the studio as soon as we wrap up in Denver. They want to get the next album out within six months."

"Jesus, Brett. The last album came out six months ago. We haven't even released all the singles yet."

Brett sat on the sofa across from him and propped his booted feet on the table. "Right. They want to keep the momentum going and have the next album ready to go as soon as we drop the last single. The only thing that keeps you on top is more music."

At the moment, he didn't care about being on top. "I need a break. Tell them I need some time off."

Brett stared at him shrewdly and Luke recognized the hungry gleam in his eyes. "Yeah. Yeah, that'll work. Your contract is up for renegotiation in a few months anyway. That way I can hold out for more money for you."

"I don't need more money. That's not the issue. I need a break."

"You absolutely need more money. You're coming off your first, sold-out, headlining tour. You've got two songs on the top twenty country music charts and an album that's been riding the top one hundred for five and a half months. I'm just looking out for your best interests."

Brett was probably right—it might be time to renegotiate his contract—but Luke wasn't as naïve as he'd been when he'd started out. More money for him meant more money for Brett. Especially since, as Luke's manager, he took twenty percent off the top.

"Whatever," Luke said. "Just get me at least two months off."

His cell phone rang and he smiled when he saw the caller ID. Right on time. "Hey, Mama."

Brett made a gesture indicating he was leaving and Luke nodded. His mama wasn't a huge fan of Brett. She thought he was a money-grubbing glory hound. She wasn't wrong, but he'd always done what was best for Luke's career—even better that it usually worked out in Brett's best interest as well.

"Hey, darlin'. Just callin' to wish you good luck tonight."

"I know, Mama. You call every night before a concert."

"At this point, it's a superstition. I feel like if I don't call, somethin' will go horribly, horribly wrong."

Luke smiled at her fancifulness but didn't tell her he thought the same thing.

"Where're you headed to next?" she asked.

"Don't you have my concert schedule taped to the fridge?" he asked.

"That's beside the point. I like to hear you tell me about it."

He took a deep breath. "Let's see. Tonight and tomorrow in

L.A., then two nights in Las Vegas, one in Phoenix, one in Albuquerque, Cheyenne, and I'll finish up in Denver."

"You sound tired."

"Yeah, a little." He slouched down into the couch and set his guitar on the cushion next to him. "Five months on the road—you get a little worn out toward the end."

"You should come home and take a break."

"I'm gonna try. As soon as we're done in Denver," he said.

"You know Rowan's still in Denver, right? Maybe you should take some time to see her."

His whole body tensed at the mention of the one person he'd been trying to avoid thinking about. Even as her image had taunted him while he'd been singing earlier.

"That's probably not a good idea, Mama. We haven't spoken to each other in years. Besides, I don't know her address." He knew Mama wouldn't let that stand. Whenever she phrased something as *maybe you should*, it meant *you're going to do it whether you like it or not*.

"I'm sure I can get her address from her parents if you wanted to drop by and say hi. I still don't understand what happened to you two. I thought for sure I'd have a bunch of grandbabies by now."

Nope. She wasn't going to let it go. "Mama."

"I know. I know. It's none of my business, but her mama doesn't know why y'all broke up either or why Rowan moved all the way out to Colorado."

"We just drifted apart." More like had swerved off in opposite directions.

"Well, I think that's a load of bad bologna. You two were as thick as thieves since you were twelve years old. You don't *just drift apart* with that kind of history."

"Mama." He thought briefly about telling her it was his fault. That he'd walked away. He'd walked toward his dream, but it had been away from her. It didn't matter that he'd thought it was only going to be for a little while—until he'd made it big and his *image* wasn't as important—he'd still picked being a hot, single country music singer over being with her.

The one regret of his life. The one dream that didn't come true.

"And who's this latest girl you've been seen with lately? Some floozy groupie you picked up at one of your concerts?"

"Please stop reading the tabloids. She's the new PR manager the label hired."

"Mmm-hmm. I know what happens backstage. I was young once too, ya know."

"Mama, I don't even want to know what you think goes on backstage other than taking pictures and signing autographs and I sure don't want to know *why* you think you know what goes on backstage."

Someone knocked on the door in the middle of the bus before it opened and his stage manager stuck his head in. "Luke, ten minutes to sound check."

He moved the phone away from his mouth. "Be right there," he called. "I gotta go, Mama."

"All right. Sing your heart out tonight. I love you."

"Love you, too. Tell everyone I said hi. Bye."

He ended the call and threw the phone back on the cushion. Pulling the drawer of the bedside table open, he pulled out his wallet. No need to carry cash or credit or a driver's license on him when he was on tour—if he wanted something, three different people would get it for him.

Lifting the inside leather flap, he took out the worn photo and brushed his thumb over the couple in the picture. Sophomore year of college. Rowan had run onto the field with everyone else when he'd scored the winning home run in the last inning of the championship game. She'd thrown her arms around his neck and he'd picked her up to kiss her. One of her friends had taken the picture at the perfect moment their mouths met.

They looked like a publicity still from some sappy romance movie. Except their story hadn't ended with them living happily ever after. A few weeks later, Brett heard him singing in a bar in Nashville. Nine months after that, Luke was a last-minute opening act for Eric Church and another three weeks on, Rowan transferred to Colorado.

It felt like he hadn't been whole since. Six years was a long time to feel like a part of you was gone.

The phone rang on the cushion next to him, startling him. Brett's face flashed across the screen.

Luke answered. "Yeah?"

"Bro. You on your way? They need you on stage."

"Be right there." Hanging up, he took one last look at the photo and returned it to its spot in his wallet before tossing it back into the drawer.

He grabbed the neck of his guitar and shoved his phone in his back pocket on the way off the bus. He needed to focus. The rest of his life would have to wait for the next six hours.

CHAPTER 4

"That makes your ass look huge."

"Too simple."

"Too fancy."

"Too much bling."

"It looks like a nightgown."

"Is that bodice see-through? What kind of person gets married in a see-through dress?"

Rowan puffed out her cheeks, stepped off the dais, and headed back to the dressing room. Debra, the poor stylist, trailed along behind her holding the heavy train.

"I'm so sorry," she said as soon as Debra closed the door.

She waved her hand. "Don't worry about it. They're not the worst family I've ever dealt with, by any stretch of the imagination."

"I find that hard to believe."

Rowan turned her back so Debra could unlace the back of the corseted dress. The one her sister had picked out because "It's just like the one I saw on that T.V. show by that one designer."

A dress Rowan would never have picked out herself. It did superb things for her waist, but the bodice was see-through from the base of the bust to the drop waist of the skirt. If she was planning on getting married in Vegas…maybe, but they were getting married in the church Michael's parents had attended for the better part of twenty years, so showing up with a see-through bodice was not going to win over the extended side of his family

"I once had a bridesmaid rip the entire front of a dress off the bride because it was the dress she'd shown the bride and told her it was the one she wanted for her wedding."

"Okay, that's kind of bad." She stepped out of the skirt and stood to the side.

"Which one do you want to try next? The lace trumpet?"

"No offense to the dress, but I don't see me wearing a trumpet style."

"How about the ruched-waist A-line?"

It was another dress her sister had picked out. It screamed over-the-top wedding. Something Adalynn had wanted for both her weddings and didn't get. Rowan must not have done a very good job of hiding her grimace because Debra let the dress fall back on the rack.

A quick knock came from the door and Debra opened it a crack, peeking her head through to see who it was. Claudia slipped in, holding a dress over her shoulder.

"A few things. First: why are you trying on all the dresses your mom and Adalynn picked out when you know you aren't going to like them? Hell, they don't even like them and they picked them out."

"Because sometimes it's easier to go along and placate them than it is to argue with them. Debra and I talked about this during the initial consultation and she picked out some dresses that are more my taste and style. I'm just getting the worst of them out of the way first."

She looked at Debra. "Not to say the dresses are bad, but they are very much my sister's style—not mine." She looked back at Claudia. "Is that another dress they picked out?"

"I'll get to that. Second, Michael is awesome. He sent over a bottle of champagne. I managed to grab the card before your mom and sister read it."

Rowan took the small white envelope and broke the seal, pulling out the handwritten note. She smiled, then read the card out loud.

"Enjoy your day. Can't wait to see the dress you pick. Hopefully your mom and sister are more bearable after a bottle of champagne." He really was the sweetest.

"I don't think you're getting any of that champagne," Claudia said. "I'm pretty sure it's going to be gone before you get out there again."

Rowan slipped the card back in the envelope and stuck it in the pocket of her purse. "Pretty sure he didn't send it for me since he knows I don't like champagne. I commented one time that they were hilarious when they drank."

"Aww. That's even sweeter," Claudia said.

"What's with the dress?" Rowan asked.

"That's one of Rafael's, isn't it?" Debra asked.

"Yes! That's the third thing. I was wandering around the store looking for dresses that didn't look like they would be featured on The Housewives of Privilege and Pretentiousness and started chatting with Rafael—he's the in-house designer—and we started talking about you and what you like and he went into his workroom, came back with this dress and said, 'This is her dress.'"

She held it in front of her body.

With a sweetheart neckline, the bodice of the dress was overlaid with delicate Chantilly lace and crystal beading. The illusion sleeves ended at the elbow and also had Chantilly lace at the shoulders and hem. An ice-blue tulle overskirt kept the satin A-line skirt from being too simple.

Rowan gently ran a finger over the lace. "It's beautiful."

Claudia's face lit up. "Put it on," she said excitedly.

Debra took the dress from her and removed it from the

hangar. She gathered it up and slipped it over Rowan's head. It was almost a perfect fit—too tight around the ribs, but a little loose in the waist. Debra clipped the dress in the back to show how it would look once properly fitted.

Rowan examined herself in the mirror, starting at the bottom of the skirt and working her way up to the neckline.

This was the dress. Classic and elegant without being over the top or ostentatious. She felt like a princess. This was the dress she would wear in a little more than four weeks when she walked down the aisle toward Michael and the rest of her life. She met her own gaze in the mirror and the next fifty years flashed before her eyes.

Kids, a house, a dog. A freaking minivan. School sports and parent-teacher conferences. Graduation and sending them off to college. She pictured all of this in her mind, but the one thing she couldn't see—the one person she couldn't see—was Michael. If she couldn't see Michael in her future, was she making the right decision?

When she'd been younger and had imagined her future, it had always been Luke. Funny enough, she had a hard time seeing him in the montage of her life. Not the superstar country singer Luke of today. Whenever she'd dreamed of her future, it had always been with the Luke of six years ago. Easygoing, always quick to make her smile, guitar-playing, Luke.

Now there was a void—a vague shape of a man, but it was like in a dream where she couldn't see the face of the person in front of her.

She wasn't sure if the blood was rushing to her head or pooling in her feet. Either way, she was light-headed and spots formed in her vision.

"Hey. Rowan. Breathe." Claudia's hand in the middle of her back snapped her out of her reverie and she inhaled sharply.

"Are you okay?"

"Yes," she said quickly. "Yes. It's beautiful." She tried to blink away the tears that inexplicably formed.

"It's perfect," Debra said. "I always know it's the right dress when the bride-to-be cries."

The dress was perfect and it was definitely the dress she was going to be married in. But she'd never been the kind of person who cried over pretty things.

CHAPTER 5

"We need to find you a date."

Luke's head snapped up. Marla didn't even look up from the tablet she had cradled in her arm, stylus tapping against the screen, after dropping that bombshell.

"What?" he asked around a mouth full of dry chicken. The catering company on this leg of the journey wasn't all that great. One month and he'd be eating his mama's homemade chicken and dumplings. He closed his eyes and imagined her drop biscuits, smothered in homemade sausage gravy. The already dry chicken turned to sawdust in his mouth and he guzzled water to make it moist enough to swallow. Appetite gone, he pushed away the plate in front of him.

"I thought I needed to be the single, eligible bachelor in order to appear attainable to the female fan base."

Marla glanced up from her tablet and gave him a look that was all too familiar—his mama had given it to him for most of his teenage years when she thought he'd said something incredibly stupid.

She looked down at her tablet, the stylus tap, tap, tapping away. She turned the screen toward him. "You're trending down with women between the ages of twenty-eight and thirty-five. They see you as the stereotypical party boy."

All he saw was a flash of some graph with a bunch of different colored lines.

"What does that matter?" Brett asked. "Young or old, women love him."

Maybe growing up with a house full of women had taught him better than most men how to interpret a look, but if Brett knew what was good for him, he'd shut his trap because he was about to get schooled.

"Women control over twenty-million dollars in worldwide spending. In the U.S., they account for eighty-five percent of all consumer purchases. More than ninety percent of women pass along deals and information to other women. Seventy percent of women use blogs to share information while almost sixty-five percent use social media. One bad comment from a social media influencer can have significantly negative effects on a product"—she looked at Luke —"or person and the trending topic on *I Was A 90s Groupie* is, 'I'm so over the bad boy cliché.'

"Which all leads to—you need a date for the charity gala at the end of next month. Preferably someone whose dress covers their ass."

Brett scoffed. "Who cares what some bored mommy house-wife with an online diary has to say?"

"That bored housewife with an online diary has half a million Instagram followers, a quarter million Facebook followers, over fifty thousand hits a day on her *diary*, and is a Luke Stone super fan. She attends every concert of his in the Northeast and we've sent her tickets to give away on her blog for the last ten shows because she is an influencer and women, who spend twenty million dollars annually, listen to her. The day after her blog post, album sales dropped by three points."

She shifted her body so her back was ever so slightly toward

Brett, effectively dismissing him from the conversation. "Who's Rowan Mitchell?"

Marla might as well have slapped him in the face with a catfish. "What?"

"She's on your friends and family list, but as far as I can tell she's the only non-family person on there. So—friend or distant relative?"

That chicken threatened to burn an acidic hole in his diaphragm and he drank some more water. "She was a friend."

"Was? But not currently?"

"Wasn't that your high school sweetheart?" Brett asked.

Marla pulled out a chair and sat at the table, two faint lines forming between her eyebrows as she looked down at her tablet.

"Wait…hang on. That was my first year with the label…" she muttered, tapping on her tablet. "Here it is. Jeez, I remember that meeting—that's when Bobby John suggested you'd sell more records if you didn't have a girlfriend. Swear to god, that was stupidest thing he'd said that week."

Luke wasn't sure if he was meant to hear that last part.

"So you don't think I should have pretended to be single?"

"What do you mean pretended? You two broke up."

"That's because she was jealous of all the attention he was getting," Brett said.

Luke glared at him. "That's not what happened."

Brett shrugged and crossed his arms. "Happens all the time. Girlfriend is supportive until she has to stand on the sidelines while the star gets all the attention and no one remembers who they are and then they get jealous.

"Plus, and I hate to be a dick by pointing this out, but your career skyrocketed after you broke up. You poured all that emotional angst into your song writing—you got your first number one single off that record. The truth is, breakups are good for hit songs."

He ignored the part about his song writing, because Brett

wasn't wrong. But he was wrong about Rowan. "Rowan didn't care that I was getting all the attention. She's not like that."

She wasn't. She'd been the one who always encouraged him—went to every one of his shows, even if it meant studying at a corner table because she had a test the next day. Rowan had convinced him to sign with Wild West Records. He wouldn't be where he was without her.

Brett shrugged his shoulders again. "Then where is she?"

"She's in Denver, as a matter of fact," Marla said. "We sent her tickets to the concert."

"You did?" Luke asked.

"That's the point of the friends and family list—it's a list of people you allow direct access to you, which also includes sending them tickets to the concert if the venue is within one-hundred miles of where they are. This is the third set of tickets we've sent her."

"Really?" Rowan had been to his concerts?

Marla gave him what he liked to refer to as her *how do you not know this?* look. At least it wasn't the *you're a dumbass* look Brett normally got.

"I don't remember ever filling out a friends and family list," Luke explained.

"You probably did it when you signed with Wild West Records and never updated it. Your manager should have done that before the beginning of the tour." She pursed her lips and rolled her eyes in Brett's direction. "I can take her off the list."

"No!" Luke jerked in his chair. "No, you can leave her on the list."

The corners of her eyes squinted as she assessed him. "It's too late now anyway, since the tickets have already been delivered. I'll make sure you review the list before your next tour. In the meantime, is there anyone else you'd like to take to the gala?"

"What's the charity?"

"Childhood literacy. One of the emcees is Laney Faith—she's

an up-and-coming singer and she's heavily involved in the charity. She's also in need of a date," Marla said. "She's got a clean, wholesome image so she'd do wonders for yours."

"Or people will think Luke dragged her over to the dark side." Brett waggled his eyebrows at his insinuation.

She shot him another scathing look. "Her image is bulletproof."

Funny thing was, Luke wasn't a party boy. He hardly even drank—even beer. When he wasn't on tour, he was usually holed up in the studio or his house in Nashville. He didn't hit the club or party scene, so he wasn't sure where the bad boy, party image had come from. Probably something Bobby John had cooked up. He'd been old school and thought any publicity was good publicity.

He lifted the baseball cap on his head, then settled it back in place. "I'll ask my sister. She's a teacher, so I know it's something she'd support. And she'd love the chance to get dressed up."

Marla stuck the stylus into her hair, twisted up on her head. "That's perfect actually. It will demonstrate to your fans that family is important and that you take the issues seriously. I'll prepare a couple of soundbites for you. If your sister's the nervous type, I can do a couple for her as well.

"I'm lining up a couple of big talk show interviews for when you come home from visiting your family and before you go back in the studio—we'll have time to figure out the rest of it and figure out a strategy."

"Yeah, sure. Whatever you think needs to be done. You're the PR person."

"Let me know when you talk to your sister and I'll send her all the details, including setting her up for a dress fitting and hair and makeup." Marla stood and left in one smooth motion.

Brett wiggled his eyebrows at Luke again as if they were in on the same joke. Luke ignored his poor attempts at humor, picked up his plate, and dropped it in the large trash can on his way out the door.

He squinted as the bright sunlight hit him and he pulled his sunglasses out of the back of his collar. Marla had stopped to talk to someone a few feet away from the door and he called out to her.

"What's wrong? Did you change your mind about taking your sister?" she asked.

He shook his head. "No, it's not about that. I was wondering if you had Rowan's phone number."

"Let me see." She worked her magic with her stylus and tablet. "There's a number with a Tennessee area code. I sent it to your email."

His phone was on the bus. "Thanks, Marla. Not just for that, but for everything you do for me. I know I don't say it enough, but you're one of the few people who manages to keep me on track."

She smiled softly. "You're welcome, Luke. Good luck with your call."

"Thanks." He half waved and strode toward his bus while his stomach turned over.

He didn't think it was the chicken this time.

Since Marla had mentioned her name, he couldn't get Rowan out of his head. Not that he needed anyone to put her in his head —she was always there, lurking in the corners of his mind.

But now…the possibility of hearing her voice was almost too much. He missed the way she used to call him *darlin'*. Maybe more than anything he missed having that connection with another person. He had his team, but he didn't have anyone who knew him inside and out.

They knew Luke Stone, chart-topping country singer. They didn't know Luke Stone, skinny kid with braces all the way up through tenth grade when he'd finally grown into his height and lost the headgear.

And now the idea of seeing Rowan, of hearing her voice,

wouldn't get out of his mind. It nagged at him like a melody for a song that wouldn't leave him alone until he'd written it down.

He still wasn't sure how things had ended so bad with Rowan. They'd agreed to the plan—they'd pretend he was single for the first year and then slowly introduce her back into his new life. He hadn't liked it any more than she had, but Bobby John and Brett had assured him that was best for his career. Singers in steady relationships didn't appeal as much to women.

Marla had blown that whole argument out of the water and Luke wondered what she would have advised if she'd been his publicist from the very beginning.

Jerking the door to his bus open, he jumped up the steps and snatched his phone from the charger. Pulling up the email app, he found Marla's message. The number was hyperlinked and he selected it.

The warning window popped up, asking if he wanted to call that number. Did he? What was he going to say? "Sorry I was an ass and listened to even bigger asses instead of doing what I knew was right?"

That was as good a place as any to start. If she didn't immediately hang up on him as soon as she heard his voice. But like his mama said, the answer's always no if you don't ask the question.

He pressed *yes* and lifted the phone to his ear.

"Who's this?" a man asked.

"Uh…this is Luke. I'm looking for Rowan."

"Sorry, man, she gave you the wrong number."

"No. This is—How long have you had this number?"

"Over three years." The guy was getting impatient.

"Okay. Thanks." He ended the call then slumped onto the bench and tapped his phone against his knee. Now what?

He had no way of finding out if she was on social media. He didn't even know what sites he was on other than Facebook because it was all handled by the PR team. He'd tried to keep his profile locked down and only have his page public, but it had gotten to the point where it was too much with everything else going on.

He opened his email again and responded to Marla's. Rowan was going to be at the Denver show. He just needed to know where she would be sitting.

CHAPTER 6

Rowan heard the front door open and close and glanced toward the short hallway as Michael set his computer bag down.

"Hey. Dinner will be ready in about ten minutes," she said.

"Sorry I'm late. Masters dropped three new accounts on my desk today." He kissed her and snagged a cracker from the package on the counter.

She playfully swatted at his hand. "I really hope you get that promotion so you don't have to work for him anymore."

"You and me both. I'm going to have to work overtime for the next three weeks to clear all my accounts so he's not calling on our honeymoon."

"As annoyed as I am that you have to work so much, I will be extremely pissed off if he calls while we're in the Keys."

"You and me both. Do I have any clothes here?"

"Yeah. There's some sweats and t-shirts in the laundry basket in the bedroom."

Michael kissed her on the cheek, rounded the end of the counter, and walked the eleven and a half steps to her bedroom.

He returned a few minutes later and opened the fridge and pulled out a beer. "Are you having wine?"

"Yes."

They fell into an easy rhythm as Michael mixed a salad together while she finished the chicken casserole, then they sat at the small kitchen table to eat.

"Have you talked to Stephanie recently?" he asked.

"Earlier today. Everything's on schedule. We're going to go to the florist tomorrow to see the samples for the bouquets. She's set up menu tasting for us next Thursday—do you think you can take a long lunch break?"

"Didn't we already to a tasting?"

"Yes, but this is for what they'll actually serve at the reception so we can make any changes or substitutions if we want."

"Thursday's not good. We have a staff meeting from eleven to one."

"Who has a two-hour staff meeting?" she asked.

"Masters. Can you take Claudia with you?" he asked.

"I'll ask her. If not, I know one of the girls at work will go with me."

"They'll probably enjoy it a lot more than I will, anyway. I don't really care what we eat," he said.

She smiled. "True. The price on that house dropped again."

"How much?"

"Three thousand."

"I'm still not excited about the price. Even with the decrease, it's significantly more than the comps in the area. Plus, we should wait until after the wedding to buy a house. Banks look more favorably on couples that are married than couples that cohabitate."

"I know, but I think we're going to have a hard time finding a house that meets both our criteria, in a good school district, and in our price range, even if it's at the high end."

"We don't have to find anything right away. We have time

before we have to start thinking about school zones." He paused with the fork halfway to his mouth, then lowered it again. "Unless there's something you need to tell me."

"What?" What he was implying clicked. "Oh! No. I'm not pregnant. It's just that we're getting married in a month and we still haven't decided whether you're moving in here or if I'm moving in with you."

"I'll move in here. My lease is up in two months and it will be less expensive to ride it out than it will be to break it. That way I also get the security deposit back."

"What about all your furniture?"

Michael finished chewing the mouth full of food. "I'll store most of it until we're ready to find a more permanent place. The rent for your apartment is less expensive than mine as well. We can split the rent here and put half of what we were both paying into an account for a down payment on a house."

Rowan stabbed a cherry tomato. "It all sounds so logical when you put it that way."

It shouldn't surprise her. He was methodical about everything, especially when it came to money.

"Has this been stressing you out?" he asked.

"A little. It's one of those things we keep saying we'll talk about but between the end of the calendar year and the beginning of tax season, you haven't had a lot of time to discuss it."

"I'm sorry, Rowan." He picked up her hand and kissed her knuckles. "I wish you'd said something earlier. I think it was one of those things I thought about discussing with you and then thought I had discussed it with you, when I hadn't—I just thought I had."

She had to smile at his circular explanation and squeezed his hand. "I understand. I know you've been busy with work."

He released her hand and scooped up another forkful of food. "I know it feels like this wedding is barreling down on us, but we have the rest of our lives to figure these things out."

"I know. It does feel like there's this catastrophic event looming on the horizon."

He chuckled. "That's one way to describe a wedding."

"That's not what I meant. It's just… It's this huge thing that has huge significance and I feel like there's going to be some sort of gatekeeper that's going to determine the rest of our lives depending on how well it goes."

"If I had known you were going to be this stressed about it, I would have suggested we elope." He took her empty plate and bowl and stacked them on top of his.

"Your mother never would have forgiven us," she said.

"She'd have gotten over it eventually." Standing, he kissed her forehead and gathered up the plates and utensils. "I've got the dishes."

"Thanks." She gazed at his back as he walked to the kitchen. He really was perfect. Sweet. Considerate. Handsome with a good paying job. She was happy and knew, no matter what, Michael would be there for her. He'd never walk away from her.

Her phone dinged with an incoming text and she picked it up. Claudia had sent a selfie of her and Maria from the concert. Rowan grinned at their obvious excitement. Her smile slipped a little when she realized they'd managed to capture the stage behind them with Luke staring down at them from the stage. She zoomed in on the picture.

Her whole body felt like it was constricting around her. She couldn't remember the last time she'd seen a picture of him. For the first year after their breakup, she'd devoured any information she could get her hands on—concert schedules, news articles, who he was dating. She'd been obsessed until she'd seen a picture of him at an awards ceremony with some cute country singer on his arm.

After eating her way through a pint of butter pecan and drinking her way through a quarter bottle of vodka, she'd gone cold turkey.

Blocked all the fan sites and pages and had a friend that worked in IT create a program that wouldn't even show her anything with his name on it.

The only thing she hadn't been able to stop were the concert tickets that were sent by special delivery every time he was in Colorado or Wyoming, but she'd never been able to bring herself to go.

She moved the picture and centered it on Claudia and Maria then noticed Claudia holding up her left hand.

Rowan zoomed in even more.

"Oh my God!" She exited to the texting app.

Are you engaged?

Yes! Didn't you read the caption?

No. I just opened the picture. OMG! I'm SO HAPPY FOR YOU!!!

She scrolled up and read the text - *I said yes!*

"What's going on?" Michael leaned over her and looked at her phone.

"Maria proposed to Claudia. Look!" She opened the picture again and he took the phone.

"Are they at the Luke Stone concert?"

Oh…right. She lost a little bit of her happiness. "Yes."

Michael handed her phone back. "You got tickets again?"

"Yes." She closed the picture.

He sat down across from her, a 'v' forming between his brows. "You didn't tell me," he said quietly.

"I didn't mean not to tell you. I was trying to find a charity to donate them to and Claudia hinted that she'd like to go, so I gave her the tickets." She smiled and shrugged. "Looks like it was a good call."

He leaned back in the chair and crossed his arms. "I can't say that it doesn't bother me that you never send them back."

She leaned forward and threaded her fingers into the hand that rested on top of his arms. "The first time I received tickets, I was going to burn them and send back the ashes."

"But you didn't."

She shook her head. "A classmate volunteered for the Make-A-Wish Foundation and mentioned there was a little boy whose wish was to go to a Luke Stone concert, but they were having a hard time reaching anyone on his management team to see if they could get tickets for him and his mom. I gave her the tickets."

"That was a coincidence."

"Kismet." She wanted to make sure he understood she wasn't holding onto the tickets for any sentimental value. "I've donated the tickets ever since. Someone should enjoy them."

"How does he know where to send them?" he asked.

"I've lived in this apartment since I moved to Colorado and I sent him my address when I first got here," she explained. "I thought maybe…"

"You'd get back together," Michael finished.

She shrugged and let go of his hand. Leaning back in her seat, she dropped her gaze to the table. "It was foolish, but I still loved him. He didn't feel the same and I eventually moved on." She raised her eyes. "A couple of years later, I met you. Things don't always work out the way you think they will when we're young, but they work out the way they're supposed to."

"What about after we get married? What are you going to do with them then?"

"What do you want me to do?"

He stared at her for several loaded seconds before uncrossing his arms and taking her hand in his. "Selfishly, I don't want you to take them but they go to a good cause."

She squeezed his hand. "It's okay to be selfish. I doubt I'll get any more after this anyway and if I do, I'll send them back."

He leaned forward and kissed her gently. "I'm beat and I have to go in for a few hours tomorrow. I'm going to bed."

"I'm going to watch a show. I'll be in there in a bit."

"Okay." He kissed her again, then retreated to the bedroom, leaving the door open a crack.

Rowan picked up her phone and opened the picture. He looked good. In jeans and a worn t-shirt with a little bit of scruff on his face, he was the poster child for bad boy country singer. He was in his element and enjoying every minute of it.

She clicked the *edit* link, cropped the picture so only Maria and Claudia were visible, and saved it to her phone.

CHAPTER 7

"*T*hank you, Denver!"

The roar of the crowd followed Luke as he left the stage. He glanced at the front row seats he'd made note of before the concert had started—the seats where Rowan should be but wasn't. He'd tried to search every face in the front of the crowd looking for her but hadn't had any luck.

Maybe Marla had been wrong about the seats that she'd been sent.

"Thanks." He took the bottle of water from the stagehand and guzzled half of it before Brett reached him.

"Great show. We've got about fifty VIPs for the meet and greet. You wanna change shirts?"

"Yeah. Real quick. I don't want to be here all night." He closed the door to the ready room and rummaged through his bag, pulling out a clean t-shirt. Pulling his soaked shirt over his head, he used a towel to wipe off the sweat, applied more deodorant, and put on the new shirt. A quick sniff test to make sure he didn't reek too badly and he was ready.

Ten minutes into the after-show, his cheeks hurt from forcing a smile for all the selfies. It'd gotten to the point where he didn't even flinch when a woman grabbed his butt or slipped something into his back pocket. He'd pull a dozen or more names and numbers out of his pockets at the end of the show. At least they weren't trying to grope his tonsils with their tongues anymore.

The two women who were in the seats Marla said had been sent to Rowan were next and he forced his smile even more.

"I love your music," the Hispanic woman said. "I know you hear that from everyone, but I would feel bad if I didn't tell you."

Her excitement was palpable whereas her companion seemed less than thrilled. She reminded him of the tolerant boyfriends who glared at him when their girlfriends gushed over him.

"Thanks. I always like to hear fans love the music." He picked up one of the headshots he signed during the VIP sessions. "Who should I make it out to?"

"Maria."

He wrote his standard statement and signed it. Handing it to her, he punished himself just a little bit more. "I noticed you two in the front row. You got engaged tonight, right?"

She beamed even more. "You saw? I was planning on doing it next week, something low-key, but when our friend gave us these tickets it seemed like the perfect moment."

"That's a really good friend—I don't think those seats are cheap."

"I didn't even think about that." She turned to her girlfriend. "Claudia, how much did Rowan pay for the tickets?"

The blonde socked her on the arm.

"Ow! What? If she paid a lot of money for the tickets, I want to pay her back."

He stepped closer and asked in a low voice, "Rowan gave you the tickets?"

The girlfriend glowered at him and pulled on Maria's arm. "Come on, we're holding up the line."

"Wait." Luke held out his arm. He didn't give a damn about the line. "How is she?"

"You know Rowan?" Maria asked.

"We were high school sweethearts." That was the easiest, least complicated explanation.

"Really?" She looked at her girlfriend. "How do I not know that?"

"I'll explain later. Let's go."

They walked away, heads close together. There was nothing he could do to keep them from leaving, short of siccing one of the security guys on them.

That was the closest he'd been to Rowan in years and he wasn't any closer to her than he'd been before. Frustrated, he turned back to the fans in line.

A few autographs and selfies later, he felt a tap on his arm.

"Excuse me, I'm sorry." Maria looked at the family next in line. "I'm so sorry. My friend wasn't feeling well and I wasn't able to get a picture. Do you mind? Real quick, I promise."

The woman looked annoyed, but said, "Sure. Go ahead."

Maria slid her hand around his waist and held up her cell-phone. "Take the piece of paper that's in my hand on your waist," she said.

He looked at her. "What?"

"Look at the phone. Claudia's in the bathroom. I told her I was getting a selfie. I've only got a few minutes, but I don't want to risk her coming out and seeing me hand you anything. So, take the piece of paper that's in my other hand and smile."

She took three quick photos while he fumbled for the piece of paper.

"What is it?" he asked.

"Rowan's number." She lowered the phone and glanced over her side toward the exit.

"Why?"

She shrugged and shook her head. "I have absolutely no idea. It's a feeling I have and I always listen to my feelings. Don't tell her where you got it and don't make me regret it."

~

LUKE STARED at the ten-digits he'd typed into his phone. All he had to do was press the green call button.

Shit.

He lowered the phone between his knees and rested his forehead in the palm of his other hand, elbow resting on his knee. What was he doing? It was almost midnight. What would he even say?

Tomorrow.

But if he waited, he knew he'd chicken out again. Better to do it now. Fast—like ripping off a bandage. Or in this case, tearing off the scab and hoping it didn't open up a vein.

He raised the phone, pressed the green button, and brought it to his ear.

Restless, he stood and paced from one end of the narrow corridor of the bus to the other. Four rings or voice mail and I'll hang up.

"Hello?"

He squeezed his eyes closed. It was the first time he'd heard her voice in years. There'd been a time when he hadn't gone more than half a day without talking to her.

"Hello?" Her voice was stronger the second time.

"Rowan?" His voice broke in the middle and he tried again. "Rowan."

The few seconds of silence stretched out into an eternity. "Luke?"

"Yeah. Hey." Heat flushed his body and sweat beaded along his hairline. He wiped the palm of his free hand on his jeans and swallowed back the emotion clogging his throat.

"How did you get this number?" she asked quietly.

He heard rustling as if she were getting out of bed. "My, uh, assistant tracked it down for me. How are you?" he asked in a rush.

"Luke…why are you calling?"

"I've been thinking about you a lot lately," he said. "I miss you, Rowan. You were the only person in my life I ever trusted completely outside my family. I—miss you."

"Luke—"

"Can I see you? I'm still in Denver. I'll come to wherever you are. Or I'll meet you somewhere. I just—I want to see you."

"I'm engaged, Luke."

His heart thumped violently in his chest. "What?"

"I'm getting married in three weeks."

He couldn't have formed words if his life depended on it.

"Luke?"

"Are you happy?"

"Yes. I'm happy. Are—Congratulations. On your awards. It's everything you ever wanted."

"I used to think that." Why hadn't she asked if he was happy? Did she just assume he was because he'd always dreamed of being a country singer? It killed him that she was congratulating him on the thing that ended up tearing them apart.

"Your fiancé—is he a good guy?" The cut kept bleeding because he kept digging in it. What he wanted to do was tell her she was supposed to be marrying him. It was always supposed to be them —Luke and Rowan. Rowan and Luke. How had everything gone so sideways?

"He is," she said.

"Would I like him?" Did it matter? He planned on hating him on principle.

"I don't know. The old Luke would have. I don't know about this Luke."

Fuuuuck. It killed him that she didn't think he was the same person he'd been before.

"I'm the same person I always was."

"I wish that were true."

"Row—"

"I have to go. Take care of yourself, Luke."

The line went dead. He stared at the blank screen before tossing it on the nightstand and falling back on the bed.

Maria had to know Rowan was getting married, so why had she given him Rowan's number? How could he even find her? Yeah, he had her address, but he didn't think she'd appreciate him showing up at her door.

He'd fooled himself for years, pretending it didn't hurt. That he was fine. That the fame and glory were worth losing the best thing in his life. For fuck's sake, he hadn't even realized she'd been the best thing in his life until it'd been too late. He could blame it on bad advice and bad management, but the truth was he let his ego and his pride drive her away because he'd been too scared to admit he needed her more than he needed the music.

Having that moment with her again, even at a distance, and having that door slammed was like losing her all over again.

CHAPTER 8

I miss you.

Why couldn't she stop thinking about those words? Three days later and that call was pretty much the only thing on her mind. His voice invaded her dreams and those words woke her from a dead sleep as if he'd whispered them in her ear while she lay in her bed.

If she didn't know better, she'd swear he'd made a deal with every radio station in the country because every single one of them seemed to be playing his songs on repeat. She'd switched over to the news station to get away from it and she hated listening to the news.

"Rowan?"

She stopped and walked backward to the reception area where Rosie, their receptionist, stood with her hand over the phone receiver.

"Cancellation or last-minute appointment?" she asked.

"Neither. It's your dad. He said he tried your cell phone, but you weren't answering," Rosie said.

Her dad? He never called her at work. "It's in my locker," she explained, taking the phone. "Dad? What's wrong?"

"Rowan...your mom's in the hospital."

She blinked and groped blindly for Rosie's chair, sitting heavily when she finally found it. "Is she okay? What happened?"

"She'd been having some stomach pain the past week or so. You know how she is...she's worse about going to the doctor than I am." He laughed softly.

"Dad—what's *wrong?*"

"They, uh...." She heard him swallow hard. "They found a mass. On one of her ovaries. She's scheduled for a biopsy in the morning, but they think—they think it might be cancer." He barely managed to say the last word.

"Shit," she whispered harshly. So many thoughts rushed through her head. Her work schedule. The wedding. She needed to call Michael. How quickly could she get a flight out? Did she have time to go home and pack a bag first? She had some gym clothes in her locker—she could always take those with her and borrow clothes from Adalynn when she got home.

Joyce Hill, the owner of the clinic, knelt beside her chair and rested a hand on her knee. Rosie must have gotten her.

"Let me make some arrangements and I'll be home as soon as I can," she told her dad. Joyce nodded her head.

"No, honey. I only called so you would know. You don't need to come home. I'm sure you're knee-deep in wedding prep—"

"Dad. I'm coming home. Send me the information for the hospital, okay?"

"Okay. If—Okay. I'll have Adalynn send it to you. Let us know when your flight arrives."

"I will. I need to go so I can make reservations. I love you, Daddy."

"Love you, too, pumpkin."

Rowan replaced the handset in the cradle and exhaled harshly.

"What do you need?" Joyce asked.

"They found a mass. My mom—" She broke off and blew out

another breath, futilely blinking back tears. They might not always see eye-to-eye, but this was her mom.

"Cancer?" Joyce asked.

She shook her head. "They don't know. They're doing a biopsy tomorrow. I'd like to be there."

"Of course." Joyce stood. "Rosie, reschedule Rowan's appointments for the rest of the week. Book them over lunch or after hours if you have to. I'll open my schedule and tell Johnathan to do the same to make sure everyone is taken care of."

Rowan's stomach dropped. "Dr. J, I don't have any more leave—I scheduled it for my honeymoon."

Her boss turned around, setting her hands on her hips, and looked down her nose. Rowan squirmed, feeling as if she'd been caught doing something that would get her grounded. Fighting the urge to confess to something—anything—she clasped her hands together.

"Rowan—this is a family dentistry. Which means we take care of family. Go do what you need to do and take care of *yours*. We'll figure out your hours when you get back."

Grateful to have an understanding boss, even if she was scolding Rowan, tears welled up again. "Thank you."

"You're welcome. Now go home and pack and check flights."

Rushing to grab her things out of her locker, she called Michael as she pushed out of the clinic with a wave to Rosie. It went to voice mail.

Damn it. "Michael, Mom's in the hospital. She's having a biopsy tomorrow. I know it's not the best timing, but I need to go home. I need to be there. Please call me when you get this."

She hit the red light leaving the shopping center and pulled up the internet app on her phone to search for flights. There was a five-thirty direct flight that would get her to Knoxville at ten-thirty with the time difference. Taking advantage of every red light, to the point of slowing down if she thought the light would turn, Rowan had her tickets booked by the time she reached her apartment. She had enough time to pack and call an Uber to take her to the airport.

Michael hadn't returned her call by the time she boarded the flight and had to turn off her phone.

It was the longest three hours of her life, or so it seemed. She tried to read, watch an in-flight movie, and sleep, but all she could think about was the possibility that her mom might have cancer.

As soon as the plane landed, she turned her phone back on and was rewarded with several texts from her dad and sister with information on her mom's surgery in the morning, and a voice mail from Michael.

"Hey, Row. Sorry to hear about your mom. I wish you'd had time to wait until I could call back, but I understand why you didn't. Call me when you land."

Slinging her satchel over her shoulder, she pulled her carry-on from the overhead bin. As soon as she reached the gate area, she called Michael.

"Hey," he answered on the first ring.

"Hey. I couldn't wait. I'm sorry," she said.

"Don't apologize—I understand. I'll call Stephanie and the minister in the morning and let them know we're postponing the wedding."

She lurched to a stop in the middle of the concourse. "What? Why?"

"Your mom's sick. I just assumed we'd postpone?"

"Shouldn't we wait to see what the prognosis is before we cancel?" That hadn't even occurred to her as an option.

"Not cancel. Postpone."

"Whatever—it's changing the date. Our wedding is less than two weeks away." She started walking again. "Let me talk to my parents and the doctor before we make that decision. Even if it's" —she inhaled deeply—"cancer, I know my mom won't want us to change the date."

"All right," he said.

She stepped onto the escalator to take her down to the rental cars and worried at the cuticle of her thumb. "Do you…? Do you want to cancel the wedding?" she asked softly.

"No. No!" He said it more forcefully the second time. "Of course not. I was only trying to help make this situation less stressful. You're absolutely right—we'll wait until you talk to your parents and the doctor."

CHAPTER 9

"*R*owan!"

Rowan sighed and dropped her head forward.

Setting her book down on the end table in the den, she called, "Yes, Mama?"

"I need you to do something."

Rolling her eyes, she pushed out of the chair, grateful her flight was tomorrow.

The tumor had been benign, but her mother was milking the doctor's orders to "take it easy" for everything it was worth. She'd only gotten out of bed to go to the bathroom and move to the couch, so finding her in the kitchen was a surprise.

"You're up," she said.

"Don't be sassy. Of course, I'm up. I can't stay in bed forever. Not all of us are on vacation."

Rowan raised her eyebrows and pressed her lips together. Yup. Her mom was definitely feeling better.

"What do you need?"

"Your father forgot his lunch. Again. I need you to take it to him."

"Sure." It would give her a chance to get out of the house. She'd agreed to help take care of her mom for a few days after she'd been released from the hospital, but being home had reminded her there was a reason she'd gone *away* to college.

Nostalgia set in on the drive to her old high school. Even being away for so long, the muscle memory took her past the dilapidated barn a mile from her parent's house, then down Main Street with its two stop lights to the high school, which was directly across the street from the combined elementary and middle school. The school's mascot, the Hollerin' Hillbilly, still boldly painted on the side of the gymnasium.

She rolled her eyes as she pulled into the visitors' parking lot, the uneasy embarrassment of being a Hollerin' Hillbilly making her neck flush. She grabbed the insulated lunch bag from the passenger seat and made her way to the front door of the school, surprised that she had to wait to be buzzed in.

The receptionist was new—at least it wasn't the same woman that had been in the position the entire time she attended Flat Holler Junior and Senior High School. She looked up from her computer with a polite smile. "Hi. Can I help you?"

"Hi. I'm here to see my dad." She held up the lunch box. "He forgot his lunch."

The woman's eyes widened. "Oh! You're Rowan! I recognize you from all the pictures on his desk. Hang on a minute and I'll see if he's free." She stood and walked to the last door on the left behind her, knocked, and poked her head in. On the way back, she spoke to a young girl waiting in one of the chairs outside the office door.

Rowan watched the girl work up a tear while the woman was looking at her, but as soon as she turned around the girl sneered at her back.

Some things never changed…mean girls especially.

"He's free. Go on back." The woman resumed her seat.

Rowan walked around the counter to her dad's office. The girl in the chair was sniffing as if she was truly crying. Rowan paused with her hand on the door handle. "Don't bother," she said.

"What?" the girl asked.

"If you think tears are going to save you, this must be your first time here. He has two daughters—tears aren't going to do anything except annoy him." She entered her dad's office, not bothering to wait for the girl's response.

"Hey, Dad."

He came around the solid wood desk. "Hey, sweetie. This is a surprise. What brings you here?"

"I brought your lunch. Mom said you forgot it."

"Oh, darn." He took the bag and placed it in the small refrigerator near the door. "This whole week has blown my routine to pieces. I feel like I'm drowning in reports."

"Isn't the Assistant Principal supposed to pick up some slack for you?" she asked, taking one of the chairs across from his desk.

"Normally, yes, but she's on her two-week training with the National Guard."

"Ooh, a military woman. I bet the students love that."

"They definitely don't get away with a lot, but the school is feeling her absence—and mine the last couple of days."

"Is that why Weeping Willow is outside?" she asked.

"Who?" He looked at the door and then nodded his head once. "Oh, yes. Allison usually handles her," he said with a sigh.

"Ah. That explains the tears. I told her not to bother since you have two daughters." She winked and smiled.

He chuckled, which was her objective. He looked stressed and worn down. The worry of the last week had taken its toll on him.

She leaned forward and rested her elbows on the edge of his desk. "Dad, would it be better for you and Mom if Michael and I postponed the wedding? It's a lot of travel and stress on top of this last week."

"What? No, of course not." He walked around the desk and pulled her up into a hug. "Your mom and I discussed that last night when I suggested she not attend and we Facetime the wedding for her. She almost bit my head off. She was very clear about the fact that even if she had cancer, she would be there to see you get married. So no, you don't need to move the wedding date." He held her away by the shoulders. "We'll both be there."

She hugged her dad tight before letting go. "Thanks, Dad. Do you mind if I walk around the school a bit?"

"Feeling nostalgic?" he asked.

She shrugged. "A little."

"Sure. Get a visitor badge from Beth. Don't want a hall monitor mistaking you for a student." He winked. "And send Jessica in."

IT REALLY HADN'T CHANGED that much. The wall murals were different, but otherwise everything was the same. She found her senior locker and, just for shits and grins, tried the combination. Feeling it catch, she banged on it twice—her trick for opening the stuck lock—and pulled it open.

The stench of old gym socks and rotted lunch hit her and she slammed it shut almost immediately. Apparently, a boy had the locker this year. Shuddering, she continued aimlessly down the hall.

Faint notes drifted from the music hall and she continued in that direction. She'd spent hours in the upper balcony doing homework while Luke had band practice after school. Except for baseball and softball season when they'd both had practice.

The door opened easily and she entered the dimly lit balcony. A few steps in, she stopped and a small gasp escaped when she saw Luke on the stage with his old music teacher.

Why didn't her dad warn her Luke was here? Had he known? Even if he had, would he have thought to warn her?

She turned slowly to sneak back out when the door she'd entered slammed shut with a loud bang. Cringing, she waited to see if they'd noticed.

"Rowan?" Luke's voice carried clearly from below.

They'd noticed.

She turned back around and walked down a few steps. "Hey. Hey, Mr. Adams." She waved, keeping most of her attention off Luke. It was impossible not to appreciate how good he looked, though. In a tight gray t-shirt and track pants with a faded Flat Holler High baseball cap, he looked like her Luke.

The thought froze her in place. Not her Luke. Not anymore.

"Hi, Rowan," Mr. Adams called up. "Here to see your dad?"

"Yes. He forgot his lunch." Why did she feel like Baby saying she carried a watermelon?

"How's your mama doin'?" he asked.

"She's a lot better, thank you. I didn't mean to interrupt. I heard the music and…I'm gonna go." She pointed over her shoulder at the door. "Sorry."

"Rowan, wait!"

She hurried to the door at the sound of Luke's voice. Yes, she was running. No, she didn't care that it made her look like a coward. She knew her limits and weaknesses. Double chocolate ganache cake—and her sweet tooth was twinging.

Luke caught up Rowan in the middle of the hall after sprinting out of the music room and up the stairs.

"Rowan. Rowan!" He grasped her elbow to slow her power walk. Thankfully, she stopped and turned.

"Hey," she said.

Hey? That was it? They hadn't seen each other in half a decade and all she had to say was hey?

"You look good," he said. She did. Her hair was longer and a little lighter. Her amber colored eyes were just as bright and deep as he remembered. She looked…curvier. Womanlier. He probably wasn't supposed to be noticing things like that but, hell, he was a guy and she had always been his ideal.

"Thanks. You do, too." She fidgeted with the hem of her t-shirt.

"How long have you been in town?"

"Only a few days. Mom had a medical scare."

"Is she okay?" He took a step closer. The pulse in the base of her neck throbbed and he heard the small, sharp intake of breath.

"Yes," she said. "The tests all came back clear. I'm actually heading home tomorrow."

Shit. That wasn't enough time. His mouth was as dry as if he'd been stuck in the desert for years and was suddenly being teased with a cold bottle of water.

Before he could say anything else, she said, "I need to go."

He grabbed her hand before she could turn around. "It was good to see you, Rowan."

She slowly pulled her fingers out of his grasp. "You, too. Take care, Luke."

Lacing his fingers on top of his head, he watched her push through the double doors leading outside and disappear. Fuck. Hearing her voice had been bad enough, but seeing her again was like a knife to the chest. It had taken everything in him not to drop to his knees and beg her forgiveness. The wariness in her eyes had gutted him. She'd never looked at him like that—as if she didn't trust him.

As if she didn't trust herself.

He dropped his hands and stared at the exit. Everything happened for a reason—he was a firm believer in that. Maybe this was life's way of telling him to take another chance. He hadn't seen or talked to her in years and now he'd done both in the space of two weeks.

A kernel of an idea formed in his head. It was crazy. So beyond stupid it wasn't funny and could very well end his career, but he was tired of wondering what if. Tired of feeling like a big chunk of him was missing.

Fortune favored the bold. And the stupid. Lord knows he'd never been accused of being a genius.

CHAPTER 10

"For the love of—If your sister walks any slower, I'll be getting married before you do," Claudia said.

Rowan peeked through the crack in the door. Adalynn wasn't even a quarter of the way down the aisle and she'd started a good thirty seconds ago.

"She is taking the step-pause instructions to extremes."

Rowan stepped away from the doors, out of the line of sight. "Even the minister looks annoyed."

"Three more steps and it's my turn," Claudia warned. "You still have time to run if you want to."

"What?"

Claudia looked over her shoulder. "Maria said I should ask you."

"Why would she tell you to do that?"

"No idea." She squinted at Rowan. "Do you?"

"No!" She pushed her shoulder. "It's your turn—go."

"Okay. I'm going." She stepped to the side and pulled open the door. "Cluck like a duck if you change your mind."

"Ducks don't cluck." Rowan gripped her bouquet and closed

her eyes. A sniffle from behind her made her glance over her shoulder.

She smiled at her dad. "Are you crying?"

He rubbed under his eyes. "It's not every day I walk my baby girl down the aisle."

"Dad…I'm not exactly a baby anymore."

"You'll always be my baby girl. Even when you have babies of your own."

Rowan kissed him on the cheek and he kissed her forehead in return. Her dad had always been a solid influence in her life. A calm in the storm of her mom and sister. She loved them, but she was more like her father than she was them and she had always been Daddy's girl. She'd thought about using Heartland's *I Loved Her First* as her processional song, but Stephanie had talked her out of it. It wouldn't have been great for pictures if her dad was bawling the whole way down the aisle. She settled for using it for the father/daughter dance instead and planned to have a fist full of tissues ready.

Stephanie stepped over to them. "Okay. It's time." She maneuvered them in front of the double doors, then moved behind Rowan to spread out the train of her dress.

The doors opened and the first notes of the traditional wedding march played. The guests stood with a loud rustle of clothing. Rowan took a deep breath and smiled what she hoped was a serene smile. With butterflies in her stomach, she stared straight ahead, her eyes on Michael. Seeing his huge grin, her smile felt more real. This was happening. She was walking to her future.

Closer to the top of the aisle, her eyes darted to Maria, standing at the end of the second row. Her easy smile didn't give away that she'd suggested Rowan run.

Why had she? She always swore by her "feelings." Rowan and Claudia might roll their eyes at her, but one of Maria's feelings was how she'd met Michael in the first place. So why had she told Claudia to ask Rowan if she was sure?

They reached the altar and Michael stepped forward. Her dad kissed her on the cheek and whispered a soft, "Love you," before he sniffled and stepped aside.

Michael took her hand, winked, and they faced the minister and stepped forward together.

~

LUKE GLARED at the entrance to the church through the windshield of the rental car. He'd figured Rowan's mom would put a wedding announcement in the paper and, sure enough, he'd found one in the *Johnson City Press*.

They'd looked good together, Rowan and her fiancé. They'd pick a candid picture for the announcement and he hated that she'd looked so happy in the picture.

He was enough of an asshole to hope she wasn't as happy as she seemed. He was also enough of an asshole to do what he was about to do.

The clock on the dash told him the ceremony began ten minutes ago. If he waited much longer, it might be too late. He shut off the engine and grabbed his guitar from the back seat. "Let's do it."

With a white-knuckle grip on the neck of his guitar, he stalked across the parking lot and into the foyer of the church. A guy in a rental tux stood in front of the double doors talking to a woman with a clipboard. Yeah, he'd been to enough award shows to recognize a rental.

"Hi. Can I help you?" the woman asked.

"Friend of the bride," Luke said.

"Sir." She gave him a once over from his old, beat-up baseball cap to his equally beat-up boots. "The ceremony has already started."

"That's all right—I'll sneak in the back."

"Dude, she said no." Rental tux stepped in front of Luke and tried to bow up.

Luke scrunched up his face. "Did you just 'dude' me?"

Cheap tux pointed toward the outside door. "Take it back outside before I take you myself."

He scoffed. "Sure thing, Keanu."

The guy drew back his elbow and fist like he was trying to win his girlfriend a stuffed bear at the county fair by hitting the punching bag hard enough.

Luke ducked and used the guy's momentum to push him to the ground. "Don't get up."

The woman tried one more time. "Sir! You can't go in—there's a wedding in progress!"

He pulled open one of the doors. "I know. I'm here to stop it."

Charging through the doors, he quickly found the Rowan. She took his breath away. He'd always thought she was beautiful but it had sharpened somehow in the last six years. In her dress and veil, with her hair cascading down her back, she was breathtaking.

Bitterness churned in his belly like acid. She should be standing up there with him. Time to fix that.

He cradled his guitar and sang the song that had poured out of him as soon as he'd made the decision to stop her wedding.

I hate to interrupt (No he didn't)
But do you believe in second chances? (Please give me one)
I'm hopelessly romantic
It's true

Our history is rough
But I think I learned some lessons
So this is my confession
To you

I know I let us both down a time or two
I'm not that guy you thought you knew
And if you're ready
Let's give this a chance again
You need to understand
I'm always gonna be your man

Rowan finally glanced at him. Her gaze was filled with trepidation. Maybe a little embarrassment. Definitely not with love and gladness at seeing him.

The groom—he refused to think of him as anything more than a prop—said something and Rowan looked back at him. She took a step closer, then the guy kissed her on the cheek, turned and walked away.

What the fuck? Luke was equal parts elated and pissed the hell off. Who the hell walks away from the woman they were getting ready to marry thirty seconds ago.

Rowan spun and rushed down the side aisle, her maid of honor close on her heels.

"Rowan!" He tried to follow her, but her dad stopped him in his tracks, her mom close behind him.

"Who the hell do you think you are?" she shouted.

"Sharon. I will handle this." Rowan's dad turned to him. "Luke. I'd like to say it's good to see you, but I'm just gonna ask what it is you think you're doing."

"Sir, I need to talk to Rowan."

Her mom leaned around her dad and pointed a finger at him. "Don't you think you should have thought about that before now?"

"Sharon."

Well aware of the audience around them, many of them filming the spectacle he'd created, he lowered his voice, hoping it wouldn't carry past the small group. "I was an idiot before. I'm man enough to admit that. I'm also man enough to make a fool of myself for the woman I love."

Adalynn chimed in. "Kind of inconvenient to figure that out right now, don't you think? What? You didn't want her until you couldn't have her?"

"It's not like that."

"Then what's it like, Lucas Stone? What's it like that you come barging into her wedding?" her mom asked.

The wedding planner rushed up to them. "The police are on the way. I've never had to call the cops on a wedding before. The reception—sure, but never the actual wedding."

Luke looked at Rowan's dad as the most reasonable person. "Mr. Mitchell?"

Before he could get a response, the planner raised her clipboard in the air and yelled, "Here! Here!"

Luke looked over his shoulder as two police officers approached from the back of the church.

"Sir, we're going to need you to come outside. Now," the first cop said.

The second cop cocked his head. "Hey. Aren't you Luke Stone?"

Luke sighed. "Yeah."

"I saw your show the other night. Great concert."

"Thanks. I'm glad you enjoyed it."

"Are you kidding me right now?" Mrs. Mitchell asked. "He interrupted my daughter's wedding! Do you know how much money we're out because of his little publicity stunt? Thousands!"

"Mrs. Mitchell, if you'll let me talk to Rowan, I'll pay you for whatever it cost."

She crossed her arms over her chest. "Damn right you will. And you're still not seeing her."

The second cop gripped Luke's elbow. "Mr. Stone, you really need to come outside so we can figure this out."

"Yeah. Fine." He gripped the neck of his guitar and sent a frustrated look in the direction Rowan had escaped. This wasn't how he'd envisioned it when he'd thought up his crazy plan. It had more of a romantic comedy feel to it in his head. She'd slap him, they'd share a passionate if not angry kiss, she'd slap him again for good measure, and then they'd run down the aisle with huge grins on their faces while the bridal party broke into an appropriately happy song.

Maybe that was going a little overboard, but it sure hadn't ended with him getting hauled off by the cops.

CHAPTER 11

Claudia followed her into the side room before Rowan could close the door, which annoyed her a little—she wanted to get away from everyone.

She settled for pacing back and forth in the small room. "I can't believe he did that."

"Which one," Claudia asked.

"Luke. Michael. Both! Both of them! Who does that? Who interrupts a wedding? Who leaves their bride at the altar? This isn't supposed to happen in real life!"

"What did Michael say?"

"That he was doing it for me." She wasn't sure she believed that. It felt more like his ego was in play, especially after their talk the night Claudia and Maria got engaged. How could he have just walked away? He'd made the decision before she'd even had time to process what was happening.

Someone knocked softly on the door and Claudia peeked through, then opened it to allow Maria to slip in.

"Did you know?" Rowan asked accusingly.

Maria stopped like a deer caught in headlights. "What?"

"Did you know Luke was going to interrupt the wedding? Is that why you told Claudia to ask me if I wanted to run?"

"No! I just…had a feeling you might be having second thoughts." She hunched her shoulders forward a little.

Making Maria feel bad made Rowan feel even crappier. Maria wouldn't sabotage her wedding on purpose.

"I'm sorry. I'm just trying to get a grip on what's happening."

"I hate to bring this up," Maria said. "But the cops are here."

Rowan threw up her hands, then pressed them to her diaphragm. Her perfectly tailored dress was suddenly too tight and felt like it was getting tighter by the second. The whole situation was pressing down on her and she couldn't catch her breath.

"I need to get out of this dress. Get me out." She tugged at the skirt and fumbled with the closure at the back. "Get me out!"

Maria and Claudia rushed to her.

"Okay. Okay. Calm down," Claudia said.

"I can't breathe," she said.

"It's loose. You're out."

Finally, the dress gave and she inhaled as if it was the first breath she'd taken after almost drowning. She pushed the fabric over her hips and stepped out of the puddle of satin and lace.

Frantically, she searched through the piles of clothes on the chairs and small couches but couldn't find her bag with the sweats and button-down she'd worn while getting her hair and makeup done.

"Here." Maria held out her overnight bag.

"Thank you." She kicked off the strappy heels she'd found on sale, stripped off the garter, and pulled on her pants and shirt.

"What do you want to do?" Claudia asked.

"I don't know. Crawl out a window and disappear for a few days."

"Are you sure?"

"Yes. I can't go out there and face all those people. All the shame and judgment. My fiancé jilted me—literally at the altar."

"No one's going to judge you," Claudia said.

Rowan straightened from shoving her things back into her bag. "Have you met my family? I don't even know half of Michael's. If I was them, I'd be judging me. I need to go somewhere to clear my head and figure out what the hell I'm supposed to do."

"It's probably a good idea anyway," Maria said. "You're starting to trend."

"What?"

She and Claudia crowded Maria to look at the Twitter app on the screen of the phone she held.

"Oh my god—I'm a hashtag!" She scrolled through the feed, finally finding the original tweet. "I'm going to kill my cousin Tanya!"

"You're not a hashtag," Claudia said.

Rowan glared at her. "Do you know anyone else who was 'hashtag: jilted' today? No? Me neither."

She dragged her feet over to one of the loveseats, shoved a bag onto the floor with a satisfying thunk, and sat down with her head on her knees.

"It's only a matter of time before I'm a meme. This is going to end up on Buzzfeed or Bored Panda or some other click-bait website."

Claudia sat next to her and wrapped an arm around her shoulders. "Don't be ridiculous. At the very least you're going to end up on TMZ. Maybe even Jimmy Fallon."

Rowan lifted her head and glared at her best friend. "Not. Helping."

"You can always go to the cabin," Maria said.

She sat up straight, dislodging Claudia's arm. "That's perfect."

Claudia shook her head. "No, it's not. My dad hasn't been up there yet. It's not stocked with anything."

"I don't care. I can stop at Walmart and get food on the way."

Claudia shifted to face her more fully. "Rowan, there's not

going to be enough fuel in the generator for more than a couple of days at the most."

"I don't care! I'll buy some extra socks and a coat and a blanket. I can get gas on the way. I have to get out of here." She grabbed Claudia's hand. "I'm clucking, Claudia. Please."

Claudia sighed. "All right."

Yes! This was perfect. She could disappear from reality for a few days until the whole thing blew over and some celebrity did or said something stupid to knock her off the trending list. She already had two weeks off from work, so no one was expecting her and she could really stay at the cabin that entire time. She'd send her dad a text to let him know she was safe—he'd understand more than anyone else her need to be alone. She could throw everything in the back of her car—her shoulders sagged.

"My car's at my house. I rode over with Adalynn this morning."

"You can take mine," Maria said.

For two weeks? Maria was quickly becoming her new favorite person. "Are you sure?"

"Of course. I'll ride back with Claudia. Let me go get my keys." She slipped out the door and closed it quietly behind her.

Rowan felt the weight of Claudia's gaze. "Stop looking at me like that."

"Are you sure this is what you want to do?"

"I need time to figure out what the hell I'm going to do and I can't do that with everyone giving me their opinion of what they think I should do, which is exactly what my mom and sister will do if I stick around."

"You don't want to try to talk to him first? Both hims?"

Rowan shook her head. "I know Michael. Once he makes a decision, he sticks to it. And...I don't know that I could get over him walking away." A tear slid down her cheek, the finality of the situation hitting her at last. "He walked away, Claudia. Without a fight."

"Oh, honey." Claudia pulled her close and leaned her head

against his. "Maybe he thinks this is what you want. What about Luke?"

"I—" She shook her head again. "I have no freaking clue."

~

THE COPS DECIDED NOT to arrest him since neither Rowan nor her family had followed them to make an official complaint. Her parents were talking to the wedding planner, who looked as flustered as a house full of hens with a new rooster. Luke wasn't sure what was going on with the groom's family.

Some of the guests had left, but most still milled around seemingly unsure of what to do. Several had gotten over the fact that he'd interrupted the wedding enough to ask to take pictures. One woman had even asked him to sign the wedding program. What the hell. Must have been one of Rowan's relatives, although he didn't recognize her.

He continued to scan the crowd, hoping to catch a glimpse of Rowan leaving, but so far no such luck. He did recognize the woman from the concert though. Her girlfriend had been the maid of honor. She appeared to be making a beeline for him and looked over her shoulder a few times. He rounded his car so it was between him and Rowan's family, in case she didn't want to be seen talking to him.

Sure enough, she rounded the back of the truck parked next to him.

"Have you talked to her? How is she?" he asked.

She didn't reply, only handed him another freaking note. What was this? Middle school?

He looked at it, then back at her. "What's this? Directions? To hell?"

She smirked. "Not quite. Rowan is going to Claudia's family's cabin for a few days to clear her head."

And she just handed him the directions to the cabin. "Why are you helping me?"

"I. Don't. Know." She gestured with her hands wide. "I just know it's supposed to happen."

Luke's brows furrowed. "What are you? Psychic?"

"Eh. Sometimes." She shrugged and walked around the back of his rental, heading in the opposite direction from where she'd come.

That was clear as mud and it all sounded hokey to him. The directions were probably to an abandoned warehouse where four hired goons were waiting to give him a beatdown. At this point, he didn't care. He'd already ignored close to a dozen calls and messages from Brett and Marla. He didn't give a damn what her motivation was as long as it got him to Rowan. Even if he did have to get a beatdown before he got there.

Lord knew he deserved it.

CHAPTER 12

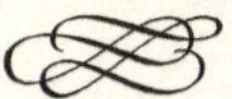

*R*owan squinted through the windshield and watched lightning streak across the sky, highlighting the thick, dark clouds. Why not add early spring thunderstorm to the list of things that happened today?

So what if there was only one thing on the list? *Ex-boyfriend objects during wedding* made for a stupendously epic, one-item list.

Fat, heavy raindrops splattered on the windshield faster than the wipers could clear it, obscuring her view of the narrow road. It'd been a couple of years since she'd been up there and the last time she'd ridden with Claudia. The headlights bore a small hole through the darkness so she barely made out the outline of the narrow bridge before she rattled over it. At least she knew she was close to the cabin. Unless there was another narrow wooden bridge over a wide creek. She leaned closer over the steering wheel and slowed to a crawl. Finally, the lights glinted on the battered *turn here if you're lost* sign.

She'd asked Claudia the first time where people turned when they weren't lost. She'd had no idea since they were never lost. Rowan knew then there was more than one way to be lost and envied her friend her confidence. Now, she knew where she was going and she still felt lost.

The road veered to the right and continued to wind through the abundant woods. Lightning cracked and lit the sky as she broke through the tree line into the clearing of the cabin. Another flash lit up the small two-bedroom cabin, giving the whole scene an ominous and creepy feeling.

"This is how horror movies start."

She pulled parallel to the door so she had only a few feet between her and being under the covered porch.

"Alone in the middle of nowhere, Rowan thought she'd reached safety when the solitary cabin came into view." She affected a dramatic movie-preview voice. "But much like Hansel and Gretel, she would soon learn appearances are always deceiving.

"Awesome. I'm freaking myself out." She grabbed her phone from the console to pull up the notes app where she'd saved the code for the lock box. Claudia had explained her dad had done that one year after they'd lost the keys and paid out the wazoo for a locksmith.

She shut off the engine and the sound of the rain pounding on the car increased. "Shoot. Maybe I should have gone to a hotel."

No. She needed this time alone. To think. To not think. To do some freaking yoga in the woods even though she never did yoga, but the idea of doing yoga at a time like this seemed like something she should consider. Even if her version of yoga was propping her fuzzy sock-clad feet up on the back porch railing while drinking coffee and wondering if there were any bears in the woods that would eat her if she decided to actually do yoga.

An involuntary shiver slithered down her back and she shook her shoulders to get rid of it. Tossing her phone and keys into one of the shopping bags, she grabbed the handles and pushed the door open. Ducking her head, she pivoted out of the car, slammed the door closed, and squealed as the rain hit her. Soaked through before she made it the four steps to the steps leading up to the porch, she used a wet sleeve to wipe the drops off her face.

She fumbled with the push-button lock, tilting it up, trying in vain to see the numbers. A bolt of lightning gave her a glimpse of the two rows and she managed to enter the code by feel. The key fell out and she poked her fingers at the door to find the lock. She used her hip to push open the door and stumbled into the cabin, leaning against the door when she closed it.

Even though she knew it was futile, she flipped the light switches next to the door. Nothing.

"Generator."

Setting the bags on the floor, she squatted and rummaged through them until she found her phone and turned on the flashlight. Staring at the phone in her hand, she looked at the door. "Why didn't you do that outside, doofus?"

She hated blonde jokes, but at the moment it was probably appropriate. At least she could blame it on stress.

Standing up, she scanned the small open room. Everything was as she remembered it, right down to the crocheted afghan on the back of the couch.

She crossed to the back door and threw the bolt, going out onto the back porch. The cool air hit her body hit her rain soaked clothes. A small door on the left end of the porch led to the attached shed that housed the generator. Her flashlight glinted off the metal lock and she stepped back inside to look for the keys. Thankfully, they hung on a hook next to the door and were even labeled.

"Instructions…instructions…" Claudia had said there was a card taped to the wall next to the door, but the wall was blank. She scanned the floor and found it tucked partway under the corner of a metal locker. Curious, she opened it and found a gas canister. Shining her light in, she found it about three-quarters full.

She turned to the generator and grimaced. She didn't even

change her own oil and now she was going to start a gas generator so she would have electricity. This was either going on today's list after she blew herself up or on the list of things she could brag about knowing how to do.

At least she had instructions—which she followed to the letter. Several minutes later, the generator was chugging away with less than half a tank of gas that would get her through three to four days if she didn't run it during most of the day.

The true test came when she flipped the light switch.

"Hurray!" She closed and locked the door, then grabbed the bags from beside the door and carried them to the small table. "Not so *Stalker in the Woods* with the lights on."

A shiver racked her body, reminding her she was still wet. She grabbed the shopping bags with the clothes she'd bought at Walmart and carried them into the bedroom, changing into a pair of cheap sweats and a zip-up hoodie. Going through the motions of unpacking the food and finding a pot and pan to make grilled cheese and soup helped her calm her nerves and settle into the cabin. It was still creepy, knowing she was alone with no one else around for miles. If this were a movie, she'd be calling herself stupid for being there. Thankfully, it wasn't a movie, and she wasn't a dumb blonde going down into the basement. Besides, if anyone had a reason to go on a murderous rampage it was her.

She carried her bowl and plate to the living room and propped her feet up on the table in front of her. Concentrating on her soup and sandwich, she avoided any deep thoughts about the day's events. There would be plenty of time to analyze everything that went wrong when she was lying in bed trying to go to sleep. Thinking about it now wouldn't stop that from happening and she'd rather do it just once.

Returning to the kitchen, she washed the bowl and plate. A loud knock at the door startled her and she dropped the soapy pot in the sink. She turned off the water and stood stock-still.

Maybe it was thunder?

Her hope died a quick death when another knock, sharper than the first, came from the door.

Oh my god! There is a serial killer!

A serial killer wouldn't knock.

Maybe not in the 1980's movie version, but the 2019 version? Absolutely.

It's probably Michael. Her Michael, not Michael Myers.

Her shoulders drooped remembering the look in his eyes right before he's walked away. It wasn't Michael.

Maybe it's a cocky, single-dad, ex-Navy SEAL-turned-lumberjack who's a secret billionaire who's lost his way in the woods along with his shirt!

"Wow. I have been reading way too much romance."

She dried her hands on the dish towel and crossed to the front door as the person on the other side knocked again. More likely it was Claudia and Maria checking on her.

Since there was no peephole or chain to verify it wasn't a serial killer, she set her foot firmly on the floor and opened the door a few inches.

"Guys, you didn't have—What are *you* doing here?"

"Rowan—" Luke stumbled forward.

Blood ran down his face from a cut on his forehead. She tried to stop his fall but couldn't hold his weight and let him fall to the floor, where he lay unmoving.

She stared down at him and pursed her lips. "I would have preferred a serial killer."

CHAPTER 13

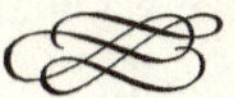

*J*esus his head hurt. And his neck and back. Luke tried to roll to his side and fell back with a groan as pain throbbed in his head. The floor probably explained why his back hurt so much.

He blinked open his eyes and stared up at the wooden door.

"You're awake. Good."

He turned his head enough to see Rowan walking across the cabin toward him with a mug.

"What happened?"

"No idea. You knocked on the door. I opened it. You fell to the floor bleeding from a cut on your head."

Rain. Sliding. Tree. Airbag.

"I slid off the road into a tree."

"Hmm." She handed him the mug and he smelled some kind of tea.

"Hmm? I tell you I slid into a tree and that's your response?"

"Here. Tylenol." She placed two tablets in his palm when he held out his hand. "I have more to say, but I'm waiting until you're not naked on the floor to ask them."

He lifted the blanket that covered him and stared down his torso. "Where are my clothes?"

"No idea. You were only wearing your underwear when you showed up."

"What?" He looked up sharply, sending shoot pain into this head. "Ow."

She stared down at him with a sardonic smile. "Serves you right. Your clothes are hanging in the bathroom. With a possible concussion already, I didn't want to add pneumonia to the list of things I had to worry about so I took your clothes off and wrapped you in a couple of blankets."

He pushed up with a groan. "If I'd known you wanted me out of my clothes, I'd have shown up sooner." His head throbbed and he felt around the worst of the pain.

"I don't want you *in* your clothes. Quit poking at it or you're going to rip it open again." She walked back toward the small kitchen as he stood.

"Did you stitch it?" He wasn't sure how he felt about her coming at him with a sharp object. The cold hit him when the blanket slipped and he wrapped it tighter around his shoulders.

"No, I found surgical glue in the first aid kit so I glued it shut and put a bandage over it." She turned sharply and leaned against the sink, crossing her arms over her chest.

Uh oh. He recognized that look. Rowan was gearing up for an argument.

"How did you know where to find me?"

"Uh…a little birdie told me?"

"Really? You had hours to come up with a plausible reason and the best you have is a birdie told you? Let me guess—that little birdie's name is Maria?"

"Don't be mad. She said she had—"

"One of her feelings." She pressed her lips together. "I wish she'd just get antacids. Why are you here, Luke?"

"I realized I may not have handled things all that well earlier today."

"You think? You interrupted my wedding. I was getting married!"

"To a guy that couldn't be bothered to fight for you. He walked away. What kind of man does that?"

Her eyes closed to slits and she glared at him. "I don't know, Luke. I remember you doing something similar, so you tell me."

"It's not the same, Row."

"Isn't it? You walked away. Seems like the same thing to me."

"You ran, Rowan. You never gave me a chance—just upped and moved to Colorado." He wanted to throw his hands up, but being naked under the blanket put him at an extreme disadvantage.

"When was I supposed to give you a chance? When some random chick had her tongue down your throat or when your manager told me your career would take off faster without me around to drag you down and that you were just too nice of a guy to break up with me?"

"That wasn't what he said. All they wanted us to do was keep our relationship on the down low until the first record was released."

She crossed her arms over her chest. "No, that's what he said when you were around. When you weren't, he made sure I knew he didn't want us together at all. Even took the time to point out how much you enjoyed the attention of all the cute little groupies that hung around after your shows."

He didn't know what she was talking about. "You were the one who told me to choose between you or my music. You issued the ultimatum, Rowan. Not me."

Shaking her head, she scoffed. "My only ultimatum was that I was your girlfriend or I wasn't. I never asked you to choose between me and your music. You did that on your own. I'm not making the same mistake twice."

She pushed away from the counter. "I'll drive you to your car in the morning to see if you can get it out of the ditch. If not, I'll drive you into town."

Stalking out of the little kitchen, she said, "Second bedroom is there. Bathroom is there. I'm turning the generator off in ten minutes so do what you need to do." She went into the bedroom she hadn't pointed at and slammed the door behind her.

Luke gripped the blanket in one hand and prodded at his forehead. That didn't go anything like he'd rehearsed in his head on the way up there. What was she talking about with Brett? When had he ever talked to her alone? And when had she ever seen a groupie try to kiss him?

Granted at the beginning, he'd been too surprised by the first couple of girls who tried to kiss him to put up much of a fight. After he'd learned to recognize the signs of a sneak attack, he'd been sure to put a safe, but still friendly, distance between him and those fans. It hadn't stopped them from copping a feel of his ass, but he eventually got used to that.

He glanced around the cozy cabin for any sign of his phone, looking by the door and on the counter with no luck. In the bathroom, he checked the pocket of his jeans which hung on the shower rod. Nothing. He hoped it was in the truck and not lying in a mud puddle along the way.

Rowan's door opened, then another door opened and closed. Figuring she was turning off the generator, he rushed to take care of business before he was forced to aim in the dark. Two seconds after he flushed, the light went out.

He waited until he heard her door close to leave the bathroom to avoid an awkward encounter. He could at least give her that right now. In the morning, she might be more receptive to listening to his reasons for stopping her wedding.

Waiting had the added benefit of giving his eyes time to adjust to the dark and he made his way out of the bathroom and into the bedroom with little problem. Once in the bedroom, his little toe found the leg of one of the twin beds. He sucked in a sharp breath.

"Damn it. Ow. Ow. Ow." Twin freaking beds. He hadn't slept in a twin bed since his first tour bus. Even the bus he had now had a full-size bed in the back and the side of the bus extended so he actually had some space in the room. He sat on the bed closest to the door and it creaked under his weight.

He crawled between the sheets and draped the blanket he'd been using over the one already on the bed.

Tomorrow was a new day and Rowan might have calmed down by then. He got it—today had been a shock and she was emotional. Hell, she'd run away from the wedding and holed up in a cabin in the middle of nowhere. He wasn't going to give up, though. He was more determined than ever to prove he was there for a second chance...and for her.

Rowan heard Luke swear, followed by the squeaking of the bed in the other room. She pounded on the pillow with a fist and smashed her head into the divot, trying to get comfortable. Not satisfied, she grabbed the other pillow and put it over her head.

It didn't matter that she couldn't hear him—she could feel him. She swore the air shifted with each breath he took. It was all in her head, but she'd always been able to feel him, especially when he was close. When they'd been together, she'd known when he walked in a room or when he walked out of it.

When he hadn't been around anymore, she'd felt that loss physically as much as she'd felt it emotionally. It was one of the reasons she'd transferred to Denver between her junior and senior year. Even just the slim possibility of running into him around Nashville had been too much to bear.

He had to go back to Nashville. She didn't know what kind of game he was playing—whether it was a publicity stunt or he needed to cover up something by having a girlfriend—but she wasn't interested. She'd take him to his car and, if it was stuck in a ditch, to the closest town on the main road. Then she'd figure out what she was supposed to do with the rest of her life.

I wonder if they need dentists in Alaska.

CHAPTER 14

*R*owan slowly blinked her eyes open and inhaled deeply. Leaning up on an elbow, she lifted the corner of the curtain and closed her eyes as pale sunlight filled the room. Squinting through one eye, she saw the clear blue sky. Bird song registered as she let the curtain go, fell back on the bed, and closed her eyes again.

"Sorry, bird, I'm not ready to face the day yet."

She must have drifted back to sleep because the next time she opened her eyes, the room felt brighter. Fully awake this time, she stretched and stared at the ceiling. This wasn't how she'd envisioned waking up today. She was supposed to wake up next to her husband so they could have a leisurely breakfast then go to the airport for their honeymoon in the Keys—not alone in a cabin in the woods with her ex-boyfriend slash wedding crasher in the next room.

Sitting up with a groan, she scratched her head. Fudge—was there coffee? She hadn't thought to get any yesterday in her mad dash through Walmart. Her focus had been on clothes to change into, clean underwear, and stuff for dinner and breakfast. Now that she wasn't in a panic to be gone from the church and her disaster of a wedding, she needed to make a list of what she needed if she was going to stay there for more than a couple of days. If her apartment wasn't so far away, she'd go home and pack more clothes.

Different clothes. Her suitcase for the beach was already packed and waiting by the door. Sundresses and bathing suits wouldn't do her much good up in the mountains. It wasn't like she had anywhere else to be today—she might as well go home after she got rid of the Destructor of Nuptials and pack enough clothes for three or four days. She could get enough gas for the generator, too. And switch cars with Maria.

She picked up her phone from the nightstand and turned it on. She'd shut it down last night because she hadn't wanted to deal with the texts and messages. It powered on and she unlocked it.

The display showed it was a little after nine and she had no bars. Hmm…she could have sworn she had one or two last night. Had the storm taken out a tower?

Eh. No biggie. It wasn't like she wanted to call anyone anyway. The more pressing concern was finding her charger because she had less than twenty percent battery left.

She pulled on the sweat pants and thick socks from last night and took a deep breath, trying to psych herself up to face the Matrimony Murderer and the possibility of no coffee.

Sticking a hair tie between her teeth, she pulled her hair into a bun and secured it with the elastic. The cabin was blessedly empty, so Luke was either outside or still asleep. She stared at the closed door of the other room and chewed at the corner of her nail.

The cut on his head hadn't been too bad, right? What if he had a concussion? She'd been too angry to think about that last night. Should she check on him? She let out a disgruntled sigh and dropped her arm to her side.

She needed to check on him.

Before she could step toward the room, the bathroom door opened and Luke exited in nothing but a towel around his waist.

"Hey. Water's really cold. I couldn't figure out how to work the unit thingy in the shower."

His tight, puckered nipples proved his statement that the water was cold.

It hadn't registered the night before how much he'd filled out since the last time she'd seen him. Playing baseball through high school and college meant he'd always been lean but in the years since she'd last seen him, he'd packed on some muscle. He didn't have a six-pack, but his abs were still defined with a dark line of hair that started just below his belly button and traveled down under the towel.

She'd always appreciated his physique and her body definitely remembered his. Her core clenched as if it was happy to see an old friend and wanted to give him a hug.

Traitor.

"Rowan?"

She blinked herself out of her stupor. "What?"

He smirked, not oblivious to her staring. "I asked if you'd found my phone last night?"

Scowling at herself, she said, "No. Your pockets were empty."

"Shit. Hopefully it's in the rental and not somewhere in the woods."

"Yeah." So what if he was still good looking? It obviously didn't hurt where his fan club was concerned. "It's a tankless water heater. The water's cold because the generator isn't on."

With no further explanation, she turned and headed to the back door. Slipping into the shoes she'd left beside the door, she went outside and started the generator. Back inside, she kicked off her shoes and rummaged through the three cabinets for any sign of coffee. In the back of one of them, she found a jar of instant coffee and generic non-dairy creamer. With a grimace, she filled the kettle and put it on the stove. She needed caffeine too much to be picky about the form it came in.

Waiting for the water to boil, she leaned against the counter and stared unseeing at the floor in front of her feet. Maybe staying at the cabin wasn't such a good idea. She needed to call her mom and dad since she'd selfishly left them holding the proverbial bag. Not that she didn't think she deserved to be selfish yesterday in the heat and embarrassment of the moment, but she couldn't make the same claim today. Today it was the day to be an adult and face the music—music Luke had made, but it was her problem. Not the wedding planner's, not her parents'…hers.

First order of business was coffee, shower, and getting rid of the Wedding Wrecker. How many monikers could she come up with?

The kettle whistled as Luke came out of the bedroom wearing the clothes he'd had on the previous day. She poured water into the two cups she'd set on the counter and handed him one when he stopped next to her.

"Thanks," he said. "You remember how I like it."

Damn it. She'd fixed his cup without even thinking about it. "It's not hard to remember you take your coffee black."

He stepped closer. "But you still remembered."

She did her best to ignore the way her skin reacted to him being so close and sipped her coffee. Not bad for instant, but she wasn't going to give up her French press.

"Rowan, about what happened—"

She moved around him. "I'm going to shower and get dressed, then take you to your car."

ROWAN CARRIED her clothes and the few belongings she'd brought with her to the car and put them on the floor in the back. Going back inside, she passed Luke standing in the middle of the cabin.

"Is there something I can help with?" he asked.

"No. I need to turn off the generator and then we can go."

"What about the food in the fridge?"

She glared at the fridge, blew out a breath, and thought seriously about leaving what little food there was just to cut down the minutes she had to spend with Luke, but she didn't know when Claudia's parents planned on visiting the cabin. They probably wouldn't appreciate being greeted by spoiled food.

"I need to get that, too."

"I'll grab it," he said.

"Sure. There's a couple of grocery bags under the sink." She grabbed the keys for the padlock and left through the back door without waiting to see if he found them.

She shut off the generator and made sure the lock was closed tight. Back inside, she hung the keys back on the hook and threw the bolt on the back door. Luke pushed opened the front door as she reached for the handle and she took a quick step back to avoid getting hit with it.

"Sorry," he said.

"It's fine. Did you get everything out of the fridge?"

"Yes. I also grabbed the trash bag and put it in the trunk of your car—I hope that's okay."

"It's fine." She wasn't annoyed he'd put the bag in her car. She was annoyed she hadn't thought to grab it and he had. Which made absolutely no sense at all—it was trash. Who cared?

She did, because even for something so insignificant, she'd had to rely on him for it. The sooner they got down the mountain, the better. "Do you have anything else you need to get?"

He rubbed the palms of his hands down his t-shirt, over the front pockets of his jeans, then around to his butt. "Nope. This is all I have."

She barely stopped herself from her initial, knee-jerk reaction of asking if he wanted to check again. They didn't have that kind

of relationship anymore. They didn't have any kind of relationship.

Instead, she gestured toward the door and her means of escape. "Let's go then."

She pulled the door closed behind them and stowed the front door key back in the lockbox. Settled into the driver's seat, she started the car and plugged her phone into the charger. Trying to ignore his warm, looming presence in the passenger seat, she turned the car toward the road.

"Now that I've got you here," he said.

She turned her head enough to look at him out of the corner of her eye.

"We need to talk about this."

"We don't need to talk about anything, Luke."

"I missed you, Rowan."

She pressed the brakes hard, forcing him to brace his hand on the dash to avoid hitting it, and the car slid on the road. "I missed you too, Luke. I missed you for a long, miserable year. I missed you every time you didn't return my calls or texts. I missed you every time you didn't answer an email. I missed you right up until the time you showed up to the Academy of Country Music awards with some up-and-coming country star on your arm and I realized I had to stop missing you. So I did.

"You don't get to barge back into my life after all this time and decide you miss me. You should have missed me when you had the chance."

Her hands clenched the steering wheel so hard her knuckles hurt and she vibrated with anger. Taking a shaky breath, she looked through the windshield and took her foot off the brake, easing down on the gas.

The tension in the car was beginning to suffocate her. She'd seen the surprise in his eyes when she'd mentioned him not answering her calls or texts. Between being homesick after transferring to UC Denver and missing Luke, she'd broken down and

tried calling, texting, and sending emails in an effort to figure out how they could make it work. All she'd gotten back was silence. Now she wondered if he'd ever gotten any of her messages.

She turned a corner and slowed to a stop. A huge freaking pine tree blocked the entire road. The trunk looked like it had been struck by lightning. Not that it mattered how it fell, it only mattered that there was no going around it.

Her eyes stung. She put the car in park and dropped her head on the steering wheel, closing her eyes as tears spilled over through her lashes.

"Rowan—"

"Get out."

"Row—"

"*Please*. Get out." She couldn't go anywhere and she didn't want to *feel* him anymore. The door opened and closed softly and she took a shuddering breath. More than anything, she wanted to be numb. To not feel the hurt, the rejection, the disappointment, or the overwhelming sense of failure.

She didn't know how long she sat there trying not to think of how off track her life had become in the last two days. Eventually, she let go of the steering wheel and rested her hands in her lap, but she kept her head on the hard circle.

The passenger door opened and closed. "Is there another road out of here?" Luke asked.

She moved her head back and forth on the steering wheel. Nope. One way in. One way out. At least until after they got across the bridge.

"Are there tools at the cabin? A chainsaw or axe?"

She shrugged her shoulders. Maybe. She vaguely remembered Claudia's dad using one during one visit, but she wasn't sure and it took too much energy to explain that to him.

"All right," he said softly. "When you're ready, head back to the cabin." He got back out of the car and left her alone.

Where else was she going to go?

CHAPTER 15

*L*uke stalked up the hard-packed dirt road, glancing over his shoulder at the car. He'd never seen Rowan like that.

He'd gotten one call from her after their fight letting him know she was transferring to the University of Colorado—he'd thought that was the end. She'd given up. Between his anger and his pride, so had he.

She'd never called him after that. Not that he knew of. Things had been crazy right around that time. His debut album hit the top ten on the country charts and he'd been swept up on the rollercoaster of concerts and interviews and publicity appearances. For a while, he reached for her. He'd turn to ask her opinion or make fun of some pretentious executive and it would take a split second before he remembered she wasn't there anymore. She was supposed to be. It was always supposed to be the two of them. Until it wasn't.

He reached the cabin and stomped up the wood stairs.

Fuck. He couldn't get in.

Spinning on his heel, he leaped down to walk back to the car to ask for the lockbox combination.

Rowan pulled into the clearing before he got a few steps. She got out of the car, unlocked the door, and entered the house without saying a word. She kicked off her shoes by the door and went into the bedroom, shutting the door behind her.

It was probably for the best right now. Anything he tried to say would be wrong and make things worse. He took the keys off the hook by the back door and went out back. He opened the shed at the end of the deck and found the generator, but no tools.

He scanned the yard and noticed a larger shed tucked back into the tree line. Inside he found a push lawnmower, a chainsaw, and, if worse came to worst, an axe. Under a shelf at the back of the shed, he discovered a half-full five-gallon gas can and poured it into the chainsaw. Hopefully, it would get him through cutting up the trunk. He grabbed the chainsaw, the axe, and the eye and ear protection he found on a peg and walked around the house to the road.

Back at the tree, he dropped the axe and put on the safety glasses and hearing protection. All he had to do was clear a path wide enough for the car to get through. The chainsaw started easily and cut through the branches at the top of the tree until he could get to the trunk without being slapped in the face by damn overgrown Christmas tree.

The scent of pine and fresh cut wood surrounded him and he fell into a rhythm of trimming and sawing, which let him clear his mind of everything but concentrating on not cutting off his own limbs. He'd forgotten how calming physical labor could be. Lord knew he didn't have to lift a finger anymore if he didn't want to.

By the afternoon he'd cut through eight sections of the trunk. The sections were larger than he'd have cut for firewood, but he just needed them small enough that he wouldn't throw out his back pulling them off the road. It was still sweat-drenching, back-breaking work and his muscles protested under the strain they weren't used to.

After pulling the last piece out of the way, he sat on one of the cut sections and glanced down at his hands, covered in scratches and sap. He hadn't thought to find a pair of gloves in the shed. Making a fist, he hissed at the pain. He looked up and stared down the road that would take them out of there and possibly take Rowan out of his life. It was a risk he had to take since keeping her locked in the cabin didn't seem like a viable option. All he could hope for was that he would be able to break through her shell and convince her to give him a chance.

He pushed up from the tree and picked up the chainsaw and the rest of the things he'd brought down. Hot, sweaty, thirsty, and in desperate need of a shower, he was no closer to figuring out how to get through to Rowan. Somewhere, someway, somehow things had gone to shit between them and he had an uneasy feeling Brett and Bobby John had something to do with it.

He returned everything to the shed the way he found it, then started the generator because he was not going to take another cold shower, no matter how welcome this one might be. For one, he needed the hot water to get the sap off his arms without removing chunks of hair.

Inside there was no sign of Rowan and the bedroom door was still closed. He hesitated with his knuckles poised over the wood, then lowered his hand. Shower, food, then talk.

He turned on the water and stripped, being careful to avoid the cut on his forehead. Taking his shirt into the shower with him, he used the bar soap to wash it as best he could. There was no way he was going to be able to sit in a car for however long it took to get back to civilization smelling himself and he sure as hell wasn't going to stink Rowan out. There wasn't much he could do about his jeans, but at least they didn't reek of B.O.

Rushing through the shower, he toweled off and pulled on his boxers and jeans as his stomach reminded him he needed to eat. He wrung out his shirt and hung it over the curtain rod to dry.

Going to the car, he pulled out the bag with the refrigerated food, a can of soup, and the bread and took them back into the kitchen. Tomato soup and grilled cheese had always been Rowan's favorite comfort food.

Once more, he hesitated with his hand over the door, then knocked sharply.

"Rowan?"

The handle turned easily and he eased the door open. She lay curled up facing away from him.

Sitting on the edge of the bed next to her hip, he could tell she was awake. "I fixed some dinner."

"I'm not hungry." Her tone was soft. Tired.

That worried him more than anger would have. "You need to eat. I got the tree clear."

Her upper body twisted and she looked at him over her shoulder. "You cleared the tree?"

It was hard to miss the way her eyes flitted to his chest, then snapped back up. "Not all of it. Just enough so the car will fit through."

"Oh."

"Do you want to eat?"

"I hadn't really thought about it."

"Come eat."

She nodded and he stood to give her space as she rolled over and slung her legs over the side of the bed.

"Where's your shirt?" she asked.

"Drying. I had to wash it."

"Why?"

"It stank." He ran a hand over his abs. Hmm…maybe he should spend a little more time working out now that he had some downtime. "Is it going to bother you? Me not having a shirt on?"

She scoffed. "No."

He fought his smile. He didn't believe her. "Good. Food."

"Okay. I'll be there in a minute."

He nodded and closed the door behind him.

She followed him less than a minute later and held out a shirt.

"Here. I found some spare clothes when I got here—this should fit."

He wanted to tease her again about his nakedness, but it was probably best not to push his luck. He pulled on the shirt while she sat in the chair next to him, tucking a leg underneath her.

He wanted to ask her about what she'd said in the car, but she seemed to have drawn into herself. She stared at her plate and chewed slowly. She looked…sad.

He'd done this to her. He was a selfish bastard and if he were a better man he'd walk away—again. But he wasn't a better man and he still believed they deserved a second chance. He *wanted* a second chance.

There'd never been anyone else in his life that he'd felt a connection to the way he did with Rowan. Even now, when she was pissed and angry at him, he felt her pull—like an invisible tether that would always connect them. He'd been stupid to walk away and to ever believe that she would walk away without a good reason.

"I think we should wait for the morning to drive to town," he said.

Her spoon paused halfway to her mouth and she lowered it back to the bowl. "Why?"

I need more time. "It'll be dark soon. I don't want to run the risk of there being another tree down or the road being washed out. It'll be safer to leave in the morning so we can see what's ahead of us."

The corners of her mouth pinched and he knew she wanted to argue with him, but it was a solid reason. She nodded and finished the rest of her dinner in silence.

Rowan cleared the dishes while he explored the bookcases in the living area. "They have Monopoly," he said. "You want to play?"

She glared at him from the sink. "I'm not playing Monopoly with you."

"Why?"

"You cheat."

"What? No, I don't."

"Yes, you do." She shut off the water and dried her hands.

He crossed his arms. "When have I ever cheated at Monopoly?"

"That time we played with Shelby and you kept moving your piece ahead spaces when you thought we weren't looking."

"That was—" He stared up at the ceiling, counting back. "That was more than fifteen years ago!"

"And we haven't played Monopoly since," she said.

"They have cribbage, do you want to play that?"

She shook her head. "I think I'm just going to go to bed."

He looked at his watch. "It's not even seven o'clock. Come on, one game…please? Don't make me read a book."

Her chest expanded as she inhaled. "Fine. One game."

Luke grabbed the board and deck of cards from the bookshelf and returned to the table, sitting across from her.

She swiped the cards. "I'll shuffle."

"I am hurt by your implication." He winked and set up the pegs on the board.

"Mmm hmm."

Rowan shuffled and dealt the cards. Picking his up, he winced when the corner of one dug into the palm of his hand, right where the skin had rubbed off.

"What?" she asked.

He shook his head. "It's nothing."

Ignoring him, she set her cards down and grabbed his hand, turning it palm up. "What happened?" she asked, doing the same with his other hand.

"Been a while since I've had to chop up a tree. I don't have any calluses on my palms anymore."

"Stay there." She pushed up from the table and walked around the small island and disappeared from sight. He heard her rummaging around in the cabinets before she reappeared and returned to the table, setting a large canvas bag on the table.

"What's this?" he asked.

"First aid kit," she said, scooting the chair next to him so close her knees bracketed one of his.

The heat from her legs embraced his and he pushed the image of them wrapped around his waist out of his mind. It didn't stop the shudder from racing up his spine as her thigh brushed his.

"Hands," she said.

"What?"

"Your hands." She looked at him expectantly. "They need to be cleaned so they don't get infected."

He glanced at his raw palms. "I washed them."

"Give me your hands." She didn't wait for his compliance but grabbed both his hands and pulled them closer to her.

She was touching him—voluntarily—what the hell was he griping about? He watched her dig through the bag and pull out several items—gauze, a small brown bottle, and bandages. The antiseptic wipes stung and he inhaled through his teeth. She shook the small brown bottle and uncapped it.

"Ah! Shit!" He jerked his hand away. He didn't know if it was whatever was in the bottle or that it was put on after the antiseptic, but it hurt like a bitch.

She yanked his hand back. "Quit being a baby." She blew on the raw skin and the sting dissipated.

Unfortunately, watching her pucker her lips and feeling her cool, soft breath on his skin caused another ache to form. He glanced down quickly to gauge how much of his lap was under the table. Probably not the best time to sport a boner.

"Thank you for clearing the tree," she said.

"There didn't seem to be any other choice. Thankfully there was a working chainsaw or we would have been hiking out of here."

"I guess one good thing came out of you following me up here —I would have been screwed by myself."

"You would have figured it out."

"Maybe."

Luke looked sharply at her. "Don't do that. You're one of the smartest and most capable people I know."

Her lips formed a semblance of a smile, but he knew she was doing it to placate him. He wasn't blowing smoke up her ass. She'd always been the one people turned to for advice and help. When had all that changed?

When you let her leave, asshole. He reached over and tucked a strand of hair behind her ear.

She closed her eyes and tilted her head. He couldn't tell if it was to get closer to his touch or farther from it.

"Please don't," she whispered.

Guess that answered that question. "Rowan—"

Her eyes popped open. "I can pretend as long as you're not touching me or looking at me like that." She looked back at his hands and covered the last sore with an adhesive bandage. "I think I'm going to go ahead and go to sleep so we can get an early start in the morning. I don't know how much fuel is left in the generator—can you please turn it off before you go to bed?"

She busied herself with cleaning up the papers and first-aid supplies without looking at him, then returned to the bag to the kitchen.

Luke opened his mouth, then slumped back in his chair when she closed the bedroom door. Shit.

CHAPTER 16

Rowan woke slowly, painfully aware of the pressure on her bladder. That's what she got for going to bed so early and for not going to the bathroom first. Closing her eyes, she pulled the blanket tighter around her shoulders and tried to ignore the urge to go along with the wind howling around the cabin.

Nope. She had to go. Whimpering at the idea of getting out of her warm cocoon, she pushed the blanket aside and swung her legs over the bed. By the time she returned, her body was racked with shivers. The temperature outside must have dropped considerably. She hurried back to bed, wrapping the blanket around her like a burrito and tried to keep her teeth from clacking like a windup toy.

Once she got cold, she always had a hard time getting warm without any additional help. She didn't know if there were any extra blankets and frankly, the idea of getting out of bed to look for some was as appealing as the idea of going out and starting the generator to get some heat going.

A soft tap at the door made her clench her jaw. If she pretended to be asleep, he'd go away.

The door opened. "Rowan? You okay?"

Her whole body shook. "Mmm hmm."

"Are you cold?" he asked.

Freezing! "No, I'm good." Her teeth picked that exact moment to chatter.

"No, you're not."

She heard him approach the bed.

Luke pushed her shoulder. "Move over."

"You're not getting in bed with me," she said through clenched teeth.

"I'm cold, too. Move over." A draft of air floated over her right before his blanket covered her head.

She grumbled in protest but scooted toward the edge of the mattress. The bed jostled when he joined her. He shoved an arm under her pillow and neck and pulled her closer, leaving her wrapped up in her blanket burrito.

His body was a furnace. She'd forgotten that, but took advantage of it and inched closer, tucking her head into the pocket of his shoulder.

"This doesn't mean anything," she whispered.

"It means we're both cold and neither of us wants to go outside to start the generator." Luke turned on his side and wrapped his other arm around her, pulling her closer. "Quit thinking and go to sleep," he mumbled.

Right. Like that was going to happen. She was in bed with Luke. Her nose was pressed into the hollow of his throat and she was trapped in her blanket and his arms. Her body might be settling into the familiarity of his, but her mind was telling her she was all kinds of a fool.

Rowan closed her eyes as his heat slowly seeped into her and her body stopped shivering. She'd roll over in a few minutes...as soon as she was all the way warm.

∼

Weird—Michael wasn't normally a cuddler, but he had one arm thrown around her and a hand cupping her ass cheek with a thigh between her legs, while her head rested on the warm skin of his chest.

Rowan blinked her eyes open slowly and stared at the music note tattoo. When did Michael get a tattoo like Luke?

Luke! She rose and rolled away, only to get tangled in the blankets and fall off the edge of the bed.

"Owww."

His head appeared over the edge, his hair adorably disheveled. "You okay?"

"Yup." She pressed her lips together.

"Forget I was here?" he asked.

"Yup."

Scratching the back of his head, he let out a big yawn. "I'll get the generator started."

He disappeared from view and she watched his bare feet walk across the room and out the door. How could he pretend they hadn't woken up together? Well, she'd woken up with him. He'd woken up to her rolling off the bed.

Had he been in boxers the whole night? Her cheeks flushed at the memory of where her thigh had been wedged and damn if her nipples didn't pucker. She pressed her palms over her breasts. She was cold—that was all.

Rowan pushed at the blankets and untangled herself as she sat up. Or maybe Luke was so used to waking up with a woman in his bed it didn't even phase him.

Why did that thought depress her so much?

By the time she dressed and finished packing the rest of her things, Luke had started breakfast and had coffee brewing.

He turned her way as she left the bathroom. "You good?"

She nodded, avoiding his gaze. She couldn't meet his eyes just then, still embarrassed from waking up wrapped around him.

"The eggs are almost done. If you want to take over, I'll finish getting dressed."

"Sure." She took the spatula from his hand and stepped into his spot. He hesitated, then walked around her. She glanced over her shoulder as he walked away, painfully aware of how well his ass filled out his jeans.

They had to get off the mountain immediately.

As soon as the door closed, Luke shoved his hand down his pants and adjusted his raging hard-on. He'd gotten it mostly under control when he'd walked outside to turn on the generator, but the damn thing had a mind of its own when it came to Rowan. As soon she'd joined him in the kitchen, it had risen up as if to say, "Here I am! Look at me!"

He'd been awake when Rowan realized she'd been draped all over him and rolled off the bed. The right thing to do would have been to ease out from under her and leave before she woke, except he'd enjoyed having her pressed against him. She'd snuggled into him in her sleep and, if the last few days were anything to go by, he was enough of an asshole to take advantage of the situation.

He hadn't meant to cop of a feel of her ass, but that had always been their position when they'd been together. Pulling on the shirt she had handed him the night before, he shoved his feet into his boots. They still had to find his car and get down the mountain, which meant he hopefully had a few hours to get her to agree to…what exactly?

That was where his plan ran dry. He wanted a future with Rowan—he could see it—but he didn't know how to get from where they were now to there. He just wanted to be there without all the in between, because he had no doubt everything in between was going to suck hairy balls.

Back in the kitchen, he ate the last of the eggs while Rowan washed the pan, then bagged the remaining food, refusing to meet his gaze the entire time.

"You ready?" he asked.

"Yeah."

"Okay. I'll shut off the generator and lock up."

"Okay."

He watched as she left through the front. Maybe getting into bed with her last night had been a mistake. He'd been so cold when he'd gotten up to pee, he'd decided to check on her to make sure she was okay. She'd been shivering so hard he'd heard her teeth chattering before he'd even cracked the door. His only thought had been to get her warm. But now, her embarrassment from waking up with him might actually be more of a barrier than her anger had been.

She was already in the car when he pulled the door shut and locked the key in the box.

"Do you want me to drive?" he asked.

She shook her head. "No, I'm good."

She turned the car toward the road once again. When they reached the tree, she slowed down even more and eased over the sawdust and wood chips. The way ahead was clear and it didn't look like anything else was going to stop them from leaving.

CHAPTER 17

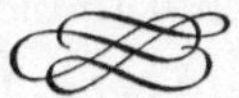

*R*owan couldn't get over the thought that she'd been just another warm body in Luke's bed. Now things were awkward and uncomfortable. She didn't know what to say or how to act so she kept her eyes on the road, resisting the urge to glance at him. To meet his gaze that she could feel on her.

This trip couldn't go fast enough.

She caught a reflection of the sunlight off something on the side of the road and blinked. She slowed to a stop and put the car in park.

"What's wrong?" Luke asked.

Pointing to the side of the road, she said, "Your truck."

"Damn. Hang tight."

"Yup."

He walked to the edge of the road and the culvert the rental was in, scratched his head, then slowly disappeared into the ditch.

So much for her hope that they'd find it in working order and she'd be able to leave him there. A few minutes later, he reappeared, scrambling back up to the road. He brushed his hands off on his jeans, adding more dirt to the layers already on them.

Looking at him through the windshield, it was hard to believe he wasn't the same Luke she'd known since she was twelve. Here, now, wearing a faded, tight-fitting t-shirt and dirt-covered jeans, he looked like her Luke. But looks were deceiving and that man was gone, replaced by someone who had a manager and a team and who didn't think twice about shaking up her life like a snow globe.

He got back in the car and immediately plugged his phone into the USB port to charge. "Well, I found my phone and my wallet, but I'm going to have to pay to get at tow truck up here to pull it out of that ditch."

Rowan nodded and shifted into drive, following the dirt packed road down the mountain. They eventually hit asphalt, signaling they were getting somewhat close to civilization. Other than Luke asking what she wanted to listen to on the radio—she didn't care—they rode in blessed, awkward silence for the rest of the trip.

Almost two hours later, she pulled into the parking lot of the Alpine Inn and Convention Center and stopped in front of reception.

"Is this okay?" she asked.

"Uh…sure. For what?"

"To leave you here. This will be easier if you call one of your people to come get you than it is for me to take you all the way back to Denver."

He turned to her in his seat. "Rowan—"

"Don't." She gripped the bottom of the steering wheel. "When we…broke up it almost broke me and I had to get away from Nashville. I went from wanting to be with you every day to being afraid I would randomly run into you. Denver seemed far enough away to get over you."

She couldn't look at him while she spoke and kept her eyes on her hands. "But I missed you so much and I knew within days that I'd made a mistake—that I shouldn't have transferred—but it was too late. So I called and texted to tell you that I was wrong and I loved you and that I wanted to find a way to make it work, that I was willing to do whatever it took to be with you. Every call that didn't get answered…every message that wasn't returned…chipped away a little bit of me each and every time until I felt like there was nothing left. It took me close to a year before I could really accept that it was over."

"Rowan, I'm not making excuses," Luke said. "But I never got any of your calls or texts. I would have answered. I realized as soon as you were gone that I'd been an asshole. Every step of the way I wanted you with me and you weren't there and that was my fault. You have to know I would have answered."

Her head jerked in a semblance of a nod. "I believe you, but it doesn't change anything that happened. I didn't think I would ever be happy again and it took me a long time to *be* happy. And up until two days ago, I was really happy." It was hard to imagine it had only been two days. "Then you stopped my wedding and undid everything I've worked for the past six years. I don't know what I'm going to do now."

She took a deep, shaky breath. "But what I do know is that I can't be with you. I can't go back to the person I was then. So, please—*don't*."

She finally looked at him. Finally let the tears that had threatened for the last two days spill over. She ached for the Luke she once knew. He placed a hand on the side of her face and ran his thumb across her cheekbone, wiping at her tears. The heat of his palm radiated out and through her body and she fought the urge to press her cheek into it. He leaned forward and pressed his lips softly against hers.

It would be so easy to fall back into him—as easy as curling into him last night had been. She closed her eyes as the memories washed over her. He had been her first kiss and she'd thought he'd be her last. But that was then.

It must have registered that she wasn't kissing him back

because he ended the kiss and pressed his forehead against hers. "I still love you, Rowan."

"I love you too, Luke. But just because you love someone doesn't mean you should be with them." She swallowed hard and pulled out of his grasp. "Please go."

He searched her gaze, shook his head slightly, and dropped his hand from her face.

"I'm not giving up, Rowan. Not this time." He grabbed his phone and got out of the car and took two steps away from it.

Her bottom lip trembled as she pulled back onto the two-lane highway that would take her to Denver. Less than half a mile down the road, she stopped the shoulder and turned on her emergency flashers. Dropping her head onto the steering wheel, her chest heaved with the first sob.

She knew this was the right decision, but why did it hurt so much?

LUKE WATCHED the taillights of Rowan's car disappear around the corner. Dierks Bentley's song, *Settle for a Slowdown*, played in his head. Other than yielding to pull onto the road, she didn't stop.

The look in her eyes had been physically painful. The hurt and devastation had glittered like shards of glass in the tears falling down her face.

He'd been wrong to think he could barge back into her life and everything would fall into place like a Hallmark Christmas movie. He knew that now. But he also knew Rowan was it for him—that his life wouldn't be complete with her in it.

He didn't plan on going anywhere and he could afford to wait days, weeks, months, hell, even years if he had to if it meant he and Rowan would be together.

The automatic doors slid open when he turned around and he approached the registration desk.

A pretty young woman smiled at him. "Good evening and welcome to the Alpine Inn."

"Thank you. Do you have any rooms available?" Not something he had considered when Rowan had asked him to get out of the car.

The clerk typed away at her computer. "We do have a few… you have your choice of a double queen or a king."

"I'll take the king." He slid his credit card and driver's license out of his wallet and passed them to her. When was the last time he'd checked himself into a hotel? He was either on the bus or someone on his team took care of it for him and handed him the key card to the room.

"Luke Stone?" The girl looked at him with wide eyes. "*The* Luke Stone?"

"Yeah." It was still weird being recognized as someone famous. He hoped he never got to the point where he expected it.

Rowan would keep you grounded and never let you forget you're from a town called Flat Holler.

"I love your music! Not as much as Miranda, 'cause Miranda's the shit, but you're my favorite male country singer."

He smiled. "Thank you. I appreciate that."

She leaned closer and said in a low voice, "Do you and your wife need some privacy? We have private cabins at the back of the property if you're trying to keep a low profile."

Not a very big fan. "I'm not married."

She leaned back as if he'd slapped her. "Oh. I thought…well, everyone thinks you and Rowan eloped."

How did she know about Rowan? "What do you mean everyone? How?"

"Mr. Stone, you're all over social media. The clip of you interrupting her wedding has over a million hits on Twitter." She sighed. "*So* romantic, but still so tragic you know? I mean, who leaves their bride standing at the altar and doesn't sock the guy interrupting in the face?"

Right?

"Although maybe not in this case, since it would have been your face." She ran his credit card and programmed two key cards while talking.

"The rumor going around is that you eloped and that's why no one has seen you. The most popular rumor is that you went to Vegas. I didn't think that was true because *someone* would have seen you and posted about it. Come to find out, you were here in Colorado all along!" She slid the room keys across the counter. "You're in room four-twenty-three."

"Thank you." He took the keys and his credit card and headed to the bank of elevators. Waiting for the car to arrive, he heard the unmistakable sound of a shutter click and knew his whereabouts would be announced to the world. He couldn't work up the energy to care.

He finally powered up his phone and waited for it to connect to the network. After eight pings, a window popped up that told him he had fifty-three unread texts. Opening the app, he quickly scrolled through. Most of them were from Marla and Brett wanting to know what the hell he'd been thinking and where the hell he was.

One text from his sister Shelby caught his eye.

Not the way I would've done it but it's about damn time.

His phone rang while he was scrolling to the latest texts and Marla's name appeared on the screen.

He hit the green dot. "Hey."

"Oh my god, you're alive." He heard the relief in her voice. "Where are you?"

"The Alpine Inn." He stepped off the elevator onto the fourth floor and followed the signs pointing to his room.

"Where is that?"

"West of Denver."

"You're still in Colorado?"

He swiped his key and pushed into the room. Bed. T.V. Shower he didn't have to charge. "Yeah."

"Have you talked to Brett?" she asked.

Ugh. He didn't want to think about what his manager was going to have to say. "Not yet. You happened to call while I was going through my messages, so I answered."

"Is Rowan with you?"

"You're the second person to ask me that question."

"Well, you interrupted her wedding and you both disappeared. It's a valid question. Even more valid: why isn't she with you?"

Luke sat at the foot of the bed and said out loud what he didn't want to admit to himself. "She didn't want me."

"And you're giving up?" she asked.

He took a breath. "No. Just taking a moment to regroup."

CHAPTER 18

*R*owan entered her apartment and shut the door, leaning against it. She was tired. Tossing her keys into the bowl on the table beside the door, she dropped the bags at her feet.

"Honey…I'm home." It would be funny if it wasn't so sad. She stared blankly ahead and tried to gather the energy to move away from the door. Dragging herself from the car had burned the last of her reserves. Her stomach grumbled, but the thought of fixing something to eat was exhausting. She didn't want to eat. She didn't want to talk to anyone, even though she needed to call her parents.

Going to the cabin had been a mistake. Not that Luke wouldn't have found her at her apartment but at least then she could have kicked him out or called the police—anything other than be stuck somewhere with him, overwhelmed by all the memories.

Seeing him again had brought back the stark reality that she missed him. It was almost as if she had regressed to that girl she'd been when they first broke up. She rubbed her forehead with the heal of a hand and grabbed the house phone on her way to the recliner. Curling up in a ball and resting her head on the arm of the chair, she dialed the number of her childhood.

Voice mail picked up. "You have reached the Mitchell residence. We have no comment. Friends and family, please call our cell phones."

"What the hell?" She ended the call and dialed her dad's cell phone.

"Rowan," he said as soon as he answered. "Thank god. Where are you?"

"I'm at home. What's going on? Why do you have that message on the house phone?"

"It's been ringing off the hook with reporters wanting an exclusive."

She covered her eyes with a hand. "I'm so, so sorry, Dad—I didn't mean to dump all this on you."

"I know, honey. Claudia explained that you went to her parents' cabin."

"Still, it wasn't fair to you or Mom or Michael's family to stick you with dealing with the fallout."

"Rowan, it's okay. I will say you missed a really good party. It was probably a good thing you guys paid for the open bar."

She huffed out a laugh his pragmatic view of the situation. "At least someone had a good time."

"Are you okay?" he asked.

"I don't know. I will be…eventually."

"Did you and Luke elope?"

"What?!" Her head jerked up. "No! Why would you ask that?"

"That's the rumor going around on the internet. You haven't seen it?"

She lowered her head to the armrest. "No. I'm avoiding my cellphone."

"Probably a good idea."

Except now she was curious what was being said.

"What are you going to do?" he asked.

Rowan shook her head. "I don't know. Probably just go into work and pretend the last two days hadn't happened." Had it really only been two days? It felt like years had passed.

"Why don't you come back home for a few days?" he asked. "You're off anyway and this time it won't be because of an emergency. You can actually visit for a few days."

"I'll think about it." That was almost the last thing she wanted to do. She loved her family, but Flat Holler, Tennessee was still the small, closed-minded town it had been when she grew up there. The last time she'd been home for an extended visit, one of her uncles had asked if she was dealing drugs since it was legal in Colorado.

"All right. Let me know what you decide so I can pick you up from the airport."

"If I decide to visit, I'll get a rental car and drive myself," she said. "How's Mom?"

"She's good. She went to Johnson City to visit Aunt Susan."

Oh, thank god.

"She wants you to call her, though."

Rowan sighed. "I'll call her tomorrow. I'm going to go to bed and sleep for the next twelve hours."

"All right, get some rest," he said. "Come home if you need to, okay?"

Tears stung the backs of her eyes. "Thanks, Daddy."

"Love you, pumpkin."

"Love you, too." She hung up and clasped the phone to her chest.

If she didn't go home, her dad would probably fly out to make sure she was okay. She didn't want to deal with all the questions, especially if the rumor was that she and Luke eloped.

Rolling off the chair, she hung up the cordless and retrieved her cell phone from her purse, powering it up on her way to the bedroom. Ten seconds after the home screen appeared, it began pinging incessantly—to the point it gave up and a text box appeared telling her she had new messages.

Eight-four texts alone. She didn't have Messenger set up for notifications, so there was no telling how many she had in there.

Sierra wanted to know why she hadn't said anything. Several other co-workers wanted to know how she knew Luke Stone and whether they'd eloped. Tomorrow would be fun if she went into work.

Claudia, Maria, her parents, and sister all wanted her to call to let them know she was okay. She'd taken care of her parents and her mom would tell Adalynn, so she thumbed Claudia's texts.

Let me know when you get there

Saw the weather rpt-did you beat the rain?

Where are you?

Are you okay?

I hope you're not answering because you don't have reception & not because you're in a ditch somewhere

Well, Luke ended up in a ditch.

Maybe we should drive up and check on you

OMG! Maria just told me what she did. I'M SO SORRY!

Maria and I are fighting. I want to check on you but she hid my keys and told me her gut said you were fine.

Seriously thinking about punching her in the gut.

P.S. Not really

Please call. We're worried.

The stream of messages continued, but Rowan hit the call button rather than reading them all.

"Where are you?" Claudia asked as soon as she answered.

"I'm home. I'm safe. We didn't elope."

"Ugh. I'd hoped you hadn't seen all that."

"I haven't. Dad told me."

"How are you really?"

"Drained. Hungry, but I don't have any food in the house. I got rid of it all because we were supposed to be gone for two weeks."

"We'll be right over—what do you want?"

Rowan didn't really want to people—even with Claudia and Maria. At the same time, she was starving and if she put them off now, they'd be there tomorrow come hell or high water.

"Pizza and ice cream." The ultimate breakup food. Might as well go for broke.

"All right. We'll be there soon."

"Okay. Let yourselves in."

"Okay. Bye."

She slipped her phone under her pillow and curled up, staring at the wall, trying not to dwell on any of the thoughts flitting through her head. Tomorrow, after she'd hopefully had a good night's sleep, would be soon enough to figure out what she should do. Whether she should try to call Michael. Whether she should go into work.

There she went thinking.

THE BED JOSTLED her awake and her eyes snapped open to find Claudia lying down in front of her.

"Hey," Claudia said.

"Hey."

Maria's arm wrapped around her waist from behind. "I'm so sorry. I really felt like it was the right thing to do."

"I'm not mad anymore," she said. "I was when he showed up, but I figure if he found me at the church, he would have found me here or at work or anywhere else if he was really determined."

"I didn't mean to hurt you," Maria said.

"I know you didn't. It wasn't too bad. I was able to say some things I'd wanted to say for a while and had never been able to." She glanced over her shoulder. "But maybe next time you get one of your feelings you can just ask for some Tums?"

Maria smiled. "I can't make any promises, but I'll try not to interfere anymore."

"Thanks." She rolled back over and faced Claudia.

"Do you know what you're going to do?" Claudia asked.

"As much as I like my current plan of avoid-at-all-costs, I can't do it forever. I can only have a pity party for so long and I can't lay around feeling sorry for myself, as fun as that sounds. I'll probably go into work tomorrow and figure out how to find out what normal looks like going forward."

"We're here if you need anything. You know that, right?"

"Yeah. Thank you."

"It might not be the right time, but…what happened between you and Luke?" Maria asked.

"You mean up at the cabin or before?"

"Both?"

"I want to know about the cabin," Claudia said.

Rowan took a deep breath and summed up from Luke showing up at the door to when she dropped him off at the hotel.

"Wow," Claudia said. "That's…"

"Obnoxious and out of line?"

"Kind of romantic…?" Maria said behind her.

"Maybe…if it had happened to anyone other than me."

They lay in silence for several minutes and Rowan soaked up the feeling of unconditional love and acceptance.

"You know," Claudia said. "This would be really hot if you were a lesbian. We could make a fortune from internet porn."

Rowan laughed at the abrupt suggestion. "I love you guys and I'm sorry to disappoint, but I'm firmly in heteroville—even though I'm about to swear off guys. I wish I was—it might make my love life easier."

"Men don't have exclusivity on being assholes," Maria said. "Love is love and no one is immune to heartbreak."

"A very sad and true statement," Rowan said.

"On that positive note," Claudia said, "we got pizza and pralines and cream ice cream. Wanna Netflix and chill?"

"As long as chill means eat our weight in pizza and ice cream and cry while we watch a Nicolas Sparks movie," Rowan said.

"What else would it mean?" Claudia asked.

"With you two? Voodoo hexes and a sacrificial virgin."

Claudia rolled out of the bed. "Like we know any virgins."

CHAPTER 19

Rowan turned into the shopping center where the dental clinic was located and pulled around back to the employee parking. She'd taken Claudia and Maria's suggestion to stay home yesterday and relax, but it had been a miserable failure. Instead of relaxing, she'd analyzed and reanalyzed everything about her relationship with Michael and where it had gone so wrong that he'd been able to walk away. She'd analyzed her nonrelationship with Luke and why, after all these years, he'd come back into it—in the middle of her wedding no less. More than anything, she'd wondered what it was about her that made it so easy for the men who supposedly loved her to walk away.

All the avoidance she'd managed had come crashing down like a house of cards. No amount of ice cream was going to fix that. She needed to be busy—to have something to occupy her mind so she couldn't think because now that she'd started to think, she couldn't stop.

Flipping down the sun visor, she checked her makeup one last time. It had taken forever to cover up the circles under her eyes. Now she only looked slightly tired instead of like she hadn't slept in four days.

Grabbing her bag from the passenger seat, she exited the car and used the remote to lock the car.

"There she is!"

She looked over her shoulder at the shout. A group of people with cameras rushed toward her from the parking lot of the sports bar directly across from the clinic. She glanced around to see who they were talking about before she realized they were talking about her.

Damn it. They must have found out where she worked from her Facebook profile. Never, ever again would she be so careless with her profile. She was still considering deleting it and being done with it completely. Direct messages from people she hadn't spoken to since high school—hell, half of them she'd never spoken to *in* high school. Complete strangers asking her personal questions she would think twice about asking her best friends. What was wrong with people?

She tucked her head down and made a beeline for the door of the clinic.

"Rowan! Rowan! Did you marry Luke Stone?"

"Rowan! Are you pregnant?"

"Rowan! How do you feel about getting left at the altar?"

"Who were you cheating on? Luke or your fiancé?"

Her mother's voice rang in her ears. *A lady does not point fingers.* She may not have been talking about the middle finger at the time, but the lesson was fitting for the situation. Besides, Rowan didn't want to give them any more reason to post unflattering pictures of her on the internet—she could only imagine what these would look like.

Not giving them the satisfaction of an answer, she swung the door to the clinic open and slipped inside, pulling it tight behind her.

"You're here." Sierra stared wide-eyed at her.

"I'm sure you've heard there was no honeymoon," she said.

"Yeah. I…uh. Sorry? I mean…let me go get Doctor Joyce. She'll want to talk to you." Sierra scurried around the desk without making eye contact.

Rowan watched her leave, then turned back to Rosie, the clinic's receptionist. "What was that about?"

"The paparazzi have been all over this clinic since we opened yesterday," she said.

Her shoulders sagged. "Awesome."

"It got so bad Doc J had to call the police to get them to vacate the premises."

"Wonderful." She crossed the reception area and pushed through the door to the examination rooms and headed directly to the lead dentist's office. There was no point in putting her things in her locker—she had a feeling she was going to have to take her time off whether she wanted it or not.

Sierra exited the office as Rowan approached and gave her a half smile, half wince. "Sorry," she whispered.

"It's okay. I should have expected something like this," Rowan said.

She knocked on the open door and stepped in.

Joyce came around her desk. "Rowan, why don't you close the door and have a seat?"

Doing as she was asked, Rowan sat on the edge of the cushioned chair.

"I know you've had some upheaval in your life over the last few days, weeks really with your mom's health scare, and I'm truly sorry for that. But this is a family business and some clients have expressed concerns about the type of attention this situation has brought to the clinic," Joyce said.

"What type of attention?" Rowan was confused. What had she missed?

"Yesterday the photographers and reporters outside made it extremely difficult for some of the patients to get in for their appointments. We were fielding so many calls, patients couldn't call in and the few that did manage to get through canceled because they didn't want to deal with it."

"But that's going to happen whether I'm here or not."

"Not if I'm able to put out a notice that you aren't working at the clinic," Joyce said.

Rowan gasped. "Are you firing me?"

Joyce reached out a hand, covering one of Rowan's. "No! Of course not. I just think it would be better if you took the time off that you were already planning to take. Maybe a few extra days until this whole thing can die down and they get distracted by the next piece of celebrity gossip."

"What if it doesn't die down?"

"We'll cross that bridge if we get to it."

That wasn't exactly encouraging, but what choice did she have? "Okay."

"Rowan, this isn't forever. I'm not firing you, but I do have to think about what's best for the practice and for the patients. Maybe this will give you some time to figure things out as well."

"Sure." In a daze, she stood and turned to leave the office.

"Do you need anything?"

Rowan shook her head. "Nope. I'm good." Since she couldn't have the one thing she needed—a distraction from her life—there wasn't anything else she needed.

"Call if you do, all right?"

She nodded and left the office, leaving without saying anything to Rosie or Sierra. It wasn't fair to them, but she couldn't handle any more looks of pity and or uncomfortable offers of help.

Bracing for the onslaught of questions, she walked as calmly as she could to her car, head down and silent. Now she understood why celebrities always wore huge sunglasses when they were out in public. She ignored the questions and got in her car, locking the doors. Checking her rearview, she backed out of the space—if they didn't want to get hit, they'd jump out of the way.

A few rushed to their cars to follow her and she made no effort to speed off. Let them follow her because she planned on driving aimlessly for as long as possible.

She couldn't go to work. Soon she might not even be able to go home, or leave home if they found out where she lived. None of this would have happened if Luke had just let the past be in the past. Who the hell did he think he was, waltzing back into her life as if she hadn't moved on? As if she hadn't been minutes away from marrying someone else? Was she a freaking toy that he had to have because someone else wanted her? Was that what this whole thing was about? He was jealous because she had finally, *finally* moved on and tried to be happy.

How dare he? And he probably wasn't dealing with half the crap she was because he probably lived in some big house with lots of security and a fence. She didn't even live in a gated complex.

The longer she drove, the angrier she became until she pulled into the parking lot of a liquor store because she was out of ice cream and vodka calories didn't count, damn it.

She stormed into the store and found the vodka aisle, grabbing a bottle of Grey Goose and a bottle of soda water. Setting the bottles down with a thud, she drummed her fingers on the counter.

"Hey, aren't you—?"

"Yes," she snapped. "I'm the woman who got left at the altar when Luke Stone interrupted my wedding. No, we didn't get married. No, I'm not pregnant. No, I don't know where he is."

The guy blushed and looked down at the bottles. "Uh, I was going to ask if you worked at Hill Family Dentistry because I think you're my dentist."

Rowan blanched and covered her face with her hands. "I'm so sorry." She dropped her hands and looked at him. "Richard, right?"

He nodded. "Yeah."

"I'm really sorry. It's been a rough couple of days. I just assumed…" She shook her head. "I'm sorry."

"It's okay. Half the people who come in here come in because they're having a bad day. Out of curiosity…who's Luke Stone?"

"You—Really?"

Richard put the bottles in paper sleeves, then in a larger bag together. "Never heard of him."

"He's a country singer," she said.

"Ah. That explains it—I'm more of a death metal fan. Thirty-five forty-seven."

She handed him her debit card.

"He really interrupted your wedding?"

"Yup."

He gave her card and the receipt back. "Wow. That's ballsy."

"Yup."

"Well, try not to drink it all at one time, okay?"

She cracked a smile. "Sure. Thanks."

"Hope your day gets better."

"Me, too." She took the bag and returned to her car, scanning for anyone with a camera. No one stood out and she hoped she had lost them while she'd driven around aimlessly. So aimlessly, she wasn't entirely sure where she was.

She set the bag on the floor behind the passenger seat and started the engine. Poor Richard. He hadn't deserved her blowup.

Luke deserved her blowup.

She snatched her phone out of her purse and scrolled through her recent calls, stopping at the unassigned number from three weeks ago.

It answered on the second ring. "Rowan?"

"Why did you do it? Why couldn't you leave well enough alone? Is your life so boring and unfulfilling that you had nothing better to do than interrupt my wedding and ruin my life? Again? I just blew up at Richard because I thought he was going to ask me if I was the woman who got left at the altar."

"Who's Richard?" he asked.

"It doesn't matter! I can't go to work because it's too disruptive to the patients. I—"

"You were fired?"

"No, I wasn't fired, but I may as well have been. The clinic owner is making me take the time off that I had scheduled for my honeymoon. Except I'm not going on my honeymoon and I have nothing else to do except sit around my house drinking ice cream and vodka floats."

"Come to Nashville."

"What? I'm not going to Nashville," she almost shouted. Did he not understand she was angry with him?

"Why not?"

"Why? Because we're not together."

"But we could be if you gave us another chance. I'm sorry this is affecting your work, but I'm not sorry about what I did. I should have done it a hell of a long time ago. Come out here. I'll put you up at a hotel if that's what you want, but I want another chance, Rowan. Let me prove to you that I'm serious."

For a dangerous millisecond—a microsecond—she considered it. What would it hurt? Would she be any worse off than she was right now? Probably. Because the last few days had shown her he could still break her heart into thousands of pieces.

"You've disrupted my life enough." She hung up the phone and tossed it onto the passenger seat.

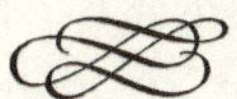

CHAPTER 20

"Mmm. There is no way he's going to be able to make that work, Tim," Rowan said. Tim Gunn left the workroom on *Project Runway* and she fast-forwarded through to the runway show. She didn't care about the drama—she had enough drama in her life—she wanted to see the dresses.

The doorbell rang and she stopped forwarding. She looked at the time on her phone, then the door, then at her pajamas. "Well, if it's the paparazzi I'll definitely be on the *what was she thinking* list."

Setting the bowl of ice cream on the table next to the recliner, she threw off the blanket, went to the door, and looked through the peephole. Michael stood on the other side, looking to the side.

Rowan rocked back on her heels. Did she want to talk to Michael? Did she want him to see her like this? Did it matter at this point anyway?

She unlocked the door and pulled it open. He looked good. A hell of a lot better than she did, that was for sure.

"Hey." He shoved his hands in the front pocket of his jeans. "Are you busy?"

"No," she said. "Just eating my feelings. You?"

He ran a hand around the back of his neck. "Do you mind if I come in? We should probably talk."

She pressed her lips together. "We probably should have done that a week ago."

"I know," he said. "There's a lot I should have said and I don't want this to be how things end between us."

She swallowed and looked at her toes. *End between us.* It was officially official. Not that it hadn't been before, but she thought… She wasn't sure what she'd thought. Or hoped for. Or wanted.

That was the biggest problem—she had no clue how to move forward. Maybe she should start by moving back.

Opening the door farther, she stepped aside with a sweep of her arm. Michael walked into the living room and sat on the edge of the couch, resting his elbows on his knees. Rowan curled back up in the chair and pulled the blanket over her lap.

His eyes flicked to the table next to her. Knowing what he saw, she said, "Welcome to the land of Wallow, where ice cream and vodka are perfectly acceptable forms of sustenance."

"Guess that's better than wallowing in bourbon and stale bar nuts."

"Is that what you did?" she asked.

"For a couple of days, yeah."

"Why?"

"Why was I wallowing?" he asked.

"Why did you walk away?" That was all she wanted to know.

"What would you have done if I'd stayed? If I'd fought for us? For you?"

"I would have married you," she said.

"Would you really have?" His gaze bore into her, searching. "I know it was an asshole thing to do, but we'd both been having doubts for a while. When he came in, it clicked in a way that it hadn't before. In a way I wasn't willing to let it. I love you, but not the way I should. Not in the way that would make me want to fight for us and know I would win. Letting you go—letting us go —was the right thing to do.

"You're still in love with him, Rowan. You've always been in love with him. I could accept that when I thought the only thing I had to compete with was his memory. I convinced myself that with enough time, you'd love me more than you loved him but while you were holding a piece of yourself back, so was I. Eventually we would have realized that."

She licked her lips and a tear rolled down her cheek. Because more than anything, the truth hurt. "I'm sorry."

"I am, too. I'm sorry that I didn't have the guts to say something before and that we ended up here."

"I do love you," she said.

"But you're not in love with me," he said.

"I—" She wasn't. How did she become that person?

"It's okay. I'm not in love with you either. I think more than anything I was in love with the perfect idea of being married and settled. It's what we're supposed to do, right? Get the promotion, the wife, have the kids, move to the suburbs. I always thought that was the goal."

She had, too. She'd thought moving on meant loving someone other than Luke. "And now? What do you want now?"

"Honestly?" he asked.

"Yes."

He cocked his head slightly. "I want to find someone who looks at me the way Luke looks at you. Someone who I'd be willing to stop a wedding for."

Rowan clenched her teeth and looked up at the ceiling to keep more tears from falling.

"Have you talked to him since then?"

"Yes." She sniffed and wiped under her nose. "He followed me up to Claudia's parents' cabin."

"How did he follow you? He was still talking to the police when I left the church."

"Maria had one of her feelings and gave him directions."

Michael scooted back on the couch. "Isn't that how we met in the first place? One of Maria's feelings?"

"As a matter of fact, it is. It was at that horrible art gallery opening she dragged me and Claudia to."

He chuckled. "That was some pretty horrific art. Who knows…maybe her feeling then was supposed to move to this feeling now and you're right where you're supposed to be."

"Kind of a screwed-up place to be."

"Yeah." They sat in silence for several seconds. "How did it end with you two? You're here. Did you leave him buried in a shallow grave behind the cabin?"

"Worse," she said. "I left him at one of those roadside inns on the highway."

He crossed a leg over the other knee. "So that's it?"

It should be, but Luke's offer was on repeat in her head like an annoying children's song that, once heard, could never be unheard.

"It's—He—I don't know. He asked me to go to Nashville."

"You have the time off."

"That's what he said."

"Are you going to go?"

"I'm not sure what good it would do," she admitted.

"Maybe you'll figure out a way to be together. Maybe you'll find out you can't stand him. But at least then you'd know."

But did she want to know?

"Can I ask something?" he asked.

"Of course."

"Why did you two really break up? All you ever said was that you wanted different things."

She swallowed hard. Years of distance didn't make the story hurt any less. Taking a deep breath, she said, "When he first signed his recording contract, it was right at the tail end of the bad-boy country singer craze. You know—a little rough around the edges, but with the hint that the right woman could put them on the straight and narrow."

Michael shrugged. He'd never listened to country music so he probably had no idea what she was talking about.

"Anyway, his manager and publicist thought they'd be able to launch him better if he appeared to be single."

"He broke up with you because his record label told him to?"

She shook her head. "Not exactly. We agreed that he would pretend to be single and I would support him from the sidelines. Except neither of us really liked the idea and we had a hard time with it. Because of school I couldn't go to all his shows, but he always made sure I had tickets to the ones I could make. One night, he was opening for some band that was supposed to be the next big thing. I had to work that night and wasn't sure if I was going to be able to make it, but I hadn't seen him in weeks and missed him so I left work early and got there after he started." She scraped at her cuticles, delaying the hard part.

"I had an all-access pass so I went backstage like I always did. He was just coming off set and this girl grabbed him and hugged him, which I didn't think anything of—he'd never given me a reason to be jealous or doubt him. Until he kissed her. Not a quick peck on the cheek like you'd give a friend or family member —full-on tonsil hockey. It was then I realized he'd taken pretending to be single to a whole other level. I was so hurt…I still remember that feeling like someone had sucker punched me in the chest. I left. He called the next day and acted like nothing had happened."

She huffed out a laugh. "He even said he missed me at the show. I told him I didn't want to pretend—we were either together or we weren't. He decided we weren't."

"And that's when you moved to Colorado?" he asked quietly.

She nodded. "I had been looking at UC Denver for dental school anyway so I just transferred for my senior year of undergrad."

"Do you think it could have been a misunderstanding?" he asked. "You were both still pretty young."

"I don't see how him making out with some girl backstage could be a misunderstanding," she said.

Michael was silent for a moment. "But now he wants another chance."

"I don't know if I can give him a second chance. I don't know that I could take being hurt like that again."

"What about you? Don't you deserve a second chance?" He leaned forward. "Rowan, I think you should go to Nashville. And I'm not just telling you that to make myself feel better.

"You should give *yourself* a second chance. Either it will work out or it won't, but if you don't go, you'll never know and one day, maybe years from now, you'll wake up wondering *what if* and it will be too late."

~

WHAT IF?

What if she went to Nashville? What if she gave Luke another chance? What if…?

She stared at her phone. All she had to do was hit the green button.

CHAPTER 21

*L*uke switched the bouquet of flowers to his left hand and wiped his right palm on his jeans. Why were flowers so awkward to hold? Scanning the faces of passengers coming down the wide hall, he chanced a glance at his watch.

Nine forty-three. Rowan's plane had touched down sixteen minutes ago—two minutes ahead of schedule. The arrivals board confirmed it. He'd never timed how long it took for him to walk from the gate area to baggage claim, but it felt like it was taking forever.

Had she gotten cold feet and decided not to come? Shit. He should have sent a driver to pick her up in Denver and take her to the airport, but she'd insisted on paying for her own plane ticket and taking a taxi.

There. He leaned to the side, trying to see around the people swarming into the arrivals area. Her dark blond hair was pulled up into a bun on top of her head. Nothing about her casual jeans and shirt should have made her stand out from the other travelers, but she still had that aura that drew his attention to her. Apparently, he wasn't the only one—several men checked her out as they passed.

The cellophane around the flowers crinkled when his fist clenched around them. He fought the urge to punch one particular guy in the face when he was a little too appreciative of Rowan's curves, especially when a pretty woman ran to hug him as he cleared the secure area. Asshole.

Weaving through the last of the group of people, he stopped short of picking Rowan up in a hug. "Hey. You made it."

She smiled softly. "I did."

"Here, I'll trade you." He thrust the flowers forward and took the handle of her small roller bag. "Do you have checked bags?"

"Just one." She smelled the bouquet. "Thank you for the flowers—you didn't have to."

Switching the bag to his other hand, he placed his palm in the small of her back to guide her toward baggage claim.

"I wanted to have something for you." He didn't admit he hadn't thought of it until he'd seen a guy holding some and had then rushed through the kiosks looking for a florist. "Although…I don't know if I have a vase at the house."

"We'll figure it out."

They reached the carousel and joined the other passengers waiting for their bags. He didn't know what to talk about or what to do with his hands. His natural inclination was to pull her against him. To press his lips to her temple. Six years ago, if they were close to each other, they were touching. Now there were only inches between them, but it felt like miles.

He cleared his throat. "How was your flight?"

She looked up at him. "It was good."

"Are you hungry? It's late so not too many restaurants will still be open, but we can stop for fast-food or I might have food at the house. Maybe. I should have food."

That got him a smile. "You're not sure if you have food?"

"Well, my housekeeper does the shopping for me, but I only got home this morning," he said.

"Where were you?" she asked.

"I was at Mama's. I always go home after a tour to decompress."

Her head nodded. "How is she? Is she still in Flat Holler?"

"She's good. I moved her to Johnson City a few years ago."

"How's Shelby?" she asked.

Luke smiled. "She's good. She's in Johnson City, too, teaching second grade. She's coming out to visit soon."

She nodded again but didn't say anything else. He was ready to talk about the weather just to keep her engaged when she stepped forward to get her suitcase.

"I got it." He reached around her and grabbed the handle, pulling it off the belt. "Is this it? It's kind of light."

"It's only a few days' worth of clothes. I wouldn't have checked a bag except I couldn't fit all my toiletries into the little bag."

"Only a few days?" He'd hoped she'd stay at least a week. She shrugged and he realized he didn't even know when she planned on leaving. He didn't want to start her visit off on an even worse foot, so he didn't ask. Guiding her through the clusters of people, he led her to the parking garage and his truck.

They were both quiet, even though they snuck glances at each other out of the corners of their eyes. He stowed her suitcase in the bed of the truck while she got in. They remained silent while exiting the garage and halfway to his house. It was uncomfortable—they'd always been able to just be with each other without feeling like they had to fill some kind of void—but he wanted to hear her voice.

"Are you tired?" he finally asked.

"No. I napped a little on the flight. I haven't had a whole lot to do other than nap for the past week. I feel like I caught up on a year's worth of sleep."

He didn't want to touch that subject since he was the reason she had so much time off.

"It's weird," she said a few minutes later.

"What's weird?" They were weird? He was weird? This whole

messed up situation was weird?

"Seeing so many familiar things, but at the same time a lot has changed."

He chanced a look at her. "Have you been back since you moved to Colorado?"

She shook her head. "No. I—I've only been back to Flat Holler."

What had she been about to say before she changed her mind? "You didn't keep in touch with anyone?"

She looked at him long and hard. "I didn't have anyone else to keep in touch with."

Breaking eye contact, he let the implication of that set it. He'd been her world and when they'd broken up, she'd had nothing to keep her there.

He took the exit that would take them to his house.

"You live in Belle Meade?"

Heat crept up the back of his neck. He'd thought about this moment in a vague I-wonder-what-Rowan-would-think kind of way, never in a real what-is-Rowan-going-to-say-when-she-sees-the-house kind of way.

"Yeah," he said.

"Do they still do the parade of homes?"

"I think so. I honestly haven't thought about that in years."

"Do you remember that one house that looked like it had a tower?"

"Vaguely," he said.

"I wonder if I can remember where it is," she said. "See if it's still as charming as I remember."

He snuck another peek out of the corner of his eye. "I think I can probably find it."

Rowan hunched over to peer out the window at the large houses they passed. Most of the houses in Belle Meade were too ostentatious for him. He'd only bought his house because it meant something.

He turned onto the wide, tree-lined street and checked the speedometer. The Belle Meade police were brutal when it came to speeding. Pulling into the drive, he held his breath.

"Oh my god! This is it!" She looked at him with a wide smile. "It's still beautiful. Classic without being overbearing like some of the other houses we passed."

She leaned back in the seat. "It beats a one-bedroom apartment, that's for sure."

"You must make decent money as a dentist," he said.

"I do, but I double up on my student loan payments so I can pay them off faster. I'd rather be debt free than living in a place that's honestly too big for me."

"Makes sense." She'd always been the more practical of the two of them. He hadn't needed to buy a house—the two-bedroom house he'd rented after moving down from Clarksville had been more than enough for him.

"We should probably go before the owner calls the cops on a couple of weirdos sitting in front of his house," she said.

"I don't think he'll mind." He pressed the button on the overhead console.

Rowan gaped at him as he waited for the garage door to open. "Are you house sitting?"

He smiled. "No."

"You own this house? You bought it?"

"I own it." He eased into the center of the three stalls.

"When? Why?" She sounded as if she didn't fully believe him—like she was waiting for the punch line.

"When—about two and a half years ago. It came on the market and I bought it. Other than mama's house, it's the only really big purchase I've made. Why…?" He closed the garage door and took a deep breath. In for a penny, in for a pound. The only way to make her believe he was serious about them was to be one-hundred-percent honest with her.

"I bought it for you. It's your house."

CHAPTER 22

Rowan stared at Luke, her jaw slack. Did he just say… "You bought me a house?"

"Well…I bought me a house, but it's your house and that's why I bought this particular house."

He wasn't making a whole lot of sense and yet she still understood him. "Luke, we weren't together two and a half years ago."

"I know, but it came on the market and I didn't want anyone else to have it." The back of his neck darkened—a sure sign he was embarrassed.

"Anyway, it was a good opportunity and a good investment. It's already increased in value," he said in a rush.

She stared after him as he got out of the truck. He'd bought the house she'd fallen in love with when all they could do was drive around on five dollars' worth of gas and dream about the day he'd make it big and he could afford to buy it for her.

He'd bought her house.

Even though they'd broken up years before.

"Are you getting out or are you going to stay in the truck?"

"What?" She looked at to her right, at Luke holding her suitcase in one hand and the passenger door open with the other. She hadn't even heard him open the door. "Oh. Yes, sorry."

The seatbelt cut across her neck. "Gah."

Luke chuckled. "It helps if you unbuckle it before you try to get out."

"Really? I like to contort myself and wriggle out of it." Now she was embarrassed. She'd been so focused on Luke's bombshell she forgot the basics of exiting a car. In her defense, no one had ever bought a house because of her. What was she supposed to do with that knowledge?

He climbed a short flight of unfinished stairs that led to a small vestibule off the kitchen.

"That's a big utility sink," Rowan said. It was low to the ground, wide, and deep.

"It's a dog washing sink." He flipped on lights as he continued through the room.

She followed him into the large kitchen. "Do you have a dog?"

"No. I'd love to have one, but I'm not home enough. It wouldn't be fair. I thought about getting one and taking it on the road, but one of the guys in my band is deathly allergic."

"That sucks. This kitchen is huge." It had to be four times the size of the kitchen in her apartment, had an eat-at counter that could seat eight people comfortably judging by the space between the bar chairs, and faced a wall of windows.

"I know. I probably only use three of the cupboards. The house is honestly too big for me, but...you know." He shrugged and turned down a short hall to what she assumed was the main entry.

"Wow. That staircase is gorgeous," she said. The dark wood matched the floors almost perfectly and gleamed. "What year was the house built?"

"Nineteen-forty, I think." He turned up the stairs. "I'll have to check."

She didn't care if it was nineteen-forty or nineteen-eighty, the craftsmanship was phenomenal. All hardwood floors and wide moldings.

She peeked into the empty living room before following him up the stairs, running her hand up the smooth banister. The colors were understated and the lack of furniture made the rooms appear huge. Turning around on the stairs, she went back down and stood in the archway between the entryway and the living room.

There was no furniture. Not even a chair. The entryway was large enough for a full-sized couch and there wasn't even a table to set his keys on.

"Rowan," he called.

Rushing up the stairs, she found him waiting at the top in a large landing that at least had a couple of couches and a table. "Why isn't there any furniture downstairs?"

He shrugged. "I don't spend any time down there, except in the kitchen."

"But you have a whole house with almost no furniture," she said to his back.

"I haven't been here a lot. It hasn't been a priority."

Who buys a house and doesn't furnish it? "Luke, why did you buy a house you don't even need?"

He stopped inside a large bedroom and turned so quickly she almost ran into him. "Because it was a link to you. However weak, however tenuous, it was a piece of you that I could still have when I didn't know if I'd ever have anything of you again."

Her heart might literally have skipped a beat.

He stepped closer, putting them toe-to-toe. "I wasn't lying when I said I missed you. I've missed you every day for the past six years." He cupped the back of her head and gazed into her eyes. "I've imagined you in every room of this house. I imagined your excitement as you bought couches and rugs and silly knick-knacks to hang on the walls. The reason it's still empty is because you weren't in it."

Rowan didn't know if she reached up or if he pulled her closer but either way, his mouth settled on hers, heavy with emotions she was only beginning to let herself feel. Desire. Desperation. Regret. Longing. So many others she couldn't put a name to.

They were two puzzle pieces fitting together. The way she wrapped her arms under his; the way he wrapped his around her shoulders, tilting her back—it was all so natural and so terrifying at the same time. Like a roller coaster she'd ridden dozens of times, but her stomach still rolled in anticipation of that first drop.

He broke the kiss, resting his forehead against hers. "I promised myself I wouldn't rush you—that I'd follow your lead. I'm sorry."

"Don't apologize," she whispered. "I would have kneed you in the nads if I'd wanted you to stop."

He chuckled and kissed her temple. "Should I wear a cup?"

She smiled. "Not yet. Maybe have one on standby, though."

"I'll keep that in mind." He rubbed her back then stepped away. "Is Chinese good? I wasn't kidding when I said I only use three of the cupboards."

"Chinese is good."

"Okay. I'll be downstairs. There's towels and stuff in the bathroom." He backed out of the room, pulling the door shut with him.

Rowan pressed a hand against her rumbling stomach. She'd been too nervous to eat on the plane and now she was hungry.

It was overwhelming. The house. Luke's confession about the house. Being back in Nashville where it all started. The walls pressed down on her and she sat on the edge of the bed. The comforter felt stiff under her hand and she leaned down and sniffed. It still had that just-out-of-the-bag smell.

She sat up and looked at the furniture. The dresser, the mirror, the bed—it was a set. Like one of those you buy from a Rooms-to-Go store, complete with lamps and artwork. On a hunch, she went to the bathroom and felt the stack of towels. They were new as well. He hadn't thought to wash them first.

He'd probably bought the bedroom set and linens not long after she'd told him she would come to Nashville because the only bed he had in the house was his. It was so considerate. So the Luke she used to know. Closing her eyes, she pressed her hand to her stomach again. Hopefully, that stomach flip was because of hunger and not because she was falling for him again.

Who was she kidding? She could be starving in the middle of a Thanksgiving feast and her stomach would still flip for Luke.

THE FLAT WHITE paint of the ceiling held no answers. Rowan should know—she'd been staring at it for the last three hours. Full of Chinese food and some local craft beer, she'd expected to fall asleep, even with her nap on the plane. No such luck. Replaying the evening in her mind, she'd tossed and turned until she finally spread out like a starfish and tried to watch the little floaties in her eyes.

Conversation had started off stilted and awkward—like a first date after a one-night stand, neither one of them sure what to say. She didn't know what she'd expected after dinner, but it hadn't been for Luke to walk her upstairs, kiss her breathless and leave her at the door to his guest room.

Who was she kidding? She'd imagined him picking her up at the bottom of the stairs and carrying her up to his bedroom like he was Rhett Butler and she was Scarlett O'Hara. She sure as hell hadn't pictured him dropping her off like she was past curfew and her dad was waiting on the other side with his hunting rifle.

Was that...? She cocked her head toward the door as if that would all of a sudden increase her ears' ability to hear. Throwing back the blanket and sheets, she tiptoed toward the door and pressed her ear to the crack. Yup. Guitar.

Giving up on sleep, she left her room and crossed the large landing, following the sound of the soft music to what must be the master bedroom. She hadn't felt right exploring earlier even though Luke told her she was welcome to.

One of the double doors was cracked and she knocked before peeking her head in. Jeez, she thought her room was big. The master took up the entire width of the house. She finally spotted Luke in a wingback chair on the other side of the undisturbed bed.

"Hey," he said. "I didn't mean to wake you."

She shook her head. "You didn't—I couldn't sleep. Can I come in?"

"Of course." He rose and leaned the neck of his guitar against his chair. "I have some water up here. Do you want me to make you some tea or something?"

"No. I can get a glass of water if I'm thirsty. Can I...?" She pointed at the blanket on the end of the bed.

"Make yourself at home." He waited until she'd curled up on the small couch across from his chair before picking up his guitar and sitting down. "Do you mind? I've got a melody going and I want to get it out."

"That's why I came in." She snuggled into the couch and laid her head against the armrest. He was brutally honest with her earlier—the least she could do was give him something in return. "I missed listening to you play."

"I missed having someone to play for all the time."

Heat crept across her chest and her stomach clenched. "Where do you see this going? Us going?"

"Forward, I hope."

"It's hard to see a way forward," she admitted.

"All I see right now is that you're really far away."

She didn't know if he meant metaphorically or right at that moment. "I can't be any closer right now."

"What will it take to get you next to me?" His fingers

continued to move over the strings, softly strumming a song she didn't recognize.

"I don't know yet," she whispered. "I'm trying to figure that out myself."

He nodded. "Thank you for coming. I meant what I said earlier—I'll do what it takes to make you believe in me—in us—again."

It was up to her. She'd taken that first free-falling step. Now she needed to follow the path ahead of her and see where it took her. To a future with Luke? Or one without him?

"Will you keep playing for me?"

"Always."

CHAPTER 23

$\mathcal{R}$owan stretched and twisted her hips, popping the kinks out of her back. Raising up to her elbows, she looked around the room. She was on top of Luke's bed, under the blanket she'd curled up on the couch with. No sign of Luke and the other side of the bed was made.

"Good, you're awake. I brought you some coffee. Still cream, no sugar, right?" Luke entered carrying two mugs.

"Yeah. Where did you sleep?"

"I took the guest bedroom." He set her coffee on the table. "If you hurry and take a shower we can get stuffed French toast before the crowd gets too thick. Think you can be ready to go in thirty minutes?"

"Uh…sure."

"Okay. Chop-chop. We've got a lot to do today." He crossed the room and entered the master bath, closing the door behind him.

Rowan picked at the crusty sleep in the corner of her eye and swung her legs over the side of the bed. Taking the coffee, she left Luke's room. Curiosity got the better of her and she detoured to look in the other bedrooms. All four were empty. Her bedroom and Luke's were the only ones with any furniture in them. A six bedroom house…for her. She sipped her coffee. It was perfect—exactly the way she liked it.

Since he wanted to leave soon, she didn't bother washing her hair and only applied basic makeup. Stuffed French toast sounded casual so she pulled on jeans and a long-sleeved t-shirt. Luke waited in the kitchen, checking his phone, when she turned the corner.

"Do you want a cup to go?" he asked.

"No, but I will take some water."

"Sure."

He filled two bottles for them to take and led her out to the garage, holding the passenger door open for her before settling into the driver's seat.

"Where are we going?" she asked.

"Sky Blue Cafe," he said, backing out of the garage. "I've heard good things about their French toast and I remember how much you liked beignets. That's all you ate when we went to New Orleans for spring break."

She smiled. "Not too many foods can beat fried dough and sugar."

He stopped at the end of the drive to check for traffic. Flashes and shouting greeted them from across the street as a small group of photographers ran across to swarm the truck.

"Assholes," Luke muttered. He pulled onto the road and sped away before they could get back in their cars.

"Does that happen a lot?" she asked.

He glanced at her. "Not usually. Especially in this neighborhood. There are a lot of big-name celebrities that live here and they all take their privacy very seriously. I think it's one of the reasons the town has its own police force instead of relying on the city or the county."

"Is it because of what happened with us?"

His eyes shone with regret. "Yes. I've never warranted that kind of attention on my own."

"Were they camping out before today?"

"When I first got home, but then I left for Johnson City. No one bothers me there."

"So they somehow know you're back and or that I'm here with you."

"Probably. I'm sure someone snapped a picture of us at the airport and posted it online somewhere. I can get ahold of my PR person and have her get it taken down."

"It doesn't matter." Rowan appreciated the gesture, but even if she was able to work that kind of magic, two more would probably go up.

"You know—I haven't had any since that trip," she said.

"What?"

"Beignets. I haven't had any since our trip to New Orleans."

The corners of his mouth rose. "Let's hope the French toast is a close substitute."

Luke parked in a garage half a block from the restaurant. When they were dating, he'd always reached for her hand when they walked together, but now it was like he actively avoided her. He touched her lower back to guide her around obstacles in their path but would remove it as soon as they were passed.

After that kiss last night and his comment that he wanted her closer, she expected him to reach for her, but he felt more like a polite, distant acquaintance than someone who wanted to be in a relationship.

Why was he holding back?

The cafe looked like any other corner diner and they were seated quickly. Rowan saw the waitress's eyes widen when she brought their waters, but she managed to tamp down her obvious excitement long enough to take their orders. At least until she pushed through the door to the kitchen. Then she let out a squeal that could be heard in the dining room.

Rowan raised her eyebrows at Luke. "Does *that* happen a lot?"

He grinned. "More and more lately. Even before...you know.

The good thing about Nashville is everyone is really low-key about seeing celebrities because they just live their lives here. They go to the grocery store, they take their kids to school, they pump their own gas. It's normal."

"You do know you're one of those *they*, right?" she asked.

He shrugged. "Not really. I think of Tim McGraw and Faith Hill, Vince Gill, or Keith Urban when I think of celebrities."

Rowan's eyes widened. "Keith Urban is married to Nicole Kidman. I love her. Do you know them? Can you invite them to dinner?"

He laughed. "Sorry, Row. I don't know them."

Her shoulders sagged. "Darn."

He kept laughing at her while he played with his straw wrapper. "I still get that way when I meet people I've looked up to my whole life."

Their plates arrived quickly and they talked while they ate. Not about anything important—how their families were doing, what friends from high school were up to, but not them. Not what was happening between them. Not what either of them expected out of her trip.

The entire day was like that. Lots of doing, not a lot of talking. Luke hadn't been kidding when he said he had a full day planned.

After breakfast he took her to the Country Music Hall of Fame, then the Ryman Auditorium for a behind the scenes tour. She'd always wanted to do it when she'd lived there but couldn't justify spending the money on it while she was in school. He bought a picnic lunch to eat on the grounds of the Parthenon, something they'd done when they were in college and too broke for the six-dollar entry fee, then they toured the art collection inside. From there she thought they were headed back to his house, possibly for a nap, but he pulled into the parking lot of the Belle Meade plantation.

Rowan rested her head against the seat for a second before pushing her door open and hopping down out of the truck and waiting for him to walk around. He laced his fingers with hers and a small frisson of electricity shot up her arm, just like it had all day, every time he'd touched her.

Every nerve ending was hyper-aware of him to the point that she felt the small hairs on her arm sway in whatever direction he was. Was it too much to ask for the two of them to spend some time alone?

She'd figured it out after the Ryman—Luke was taking her to all the places they talked about going when they were poor college students only worried about having enough money for gas to drive between Clarksville, where he'd gone to school, and Nashville, where she'd gone to school. He seemed so excited to take her everywhere that she didn't want to burst his bubble, but she wanted to spend time with just Luke—not spend hours at tourist attractions.

They joined a group getting ready to go through the house and followed along. Rowan admitted the history was interesting, even if she did have a visceral objection to it as a slaveholder plantation. Halfway through the tour, a few girls started whispering and looking their way. He had been recognized again. They made it all the way to the end of the tour before they approached en masse.

"Hi. Are you Luke Stone?" one of the girls asked, eyes wide and bright.

"I am," he said.

"Oh my gosh. We love you. I mean…we're really big fans," another girl said.

"Can we get a picture?"

"Sure." He joined the girls and took one of their cell phones to take a selfie.

"Here." Rowan held out her hand. "I can take a picture with everyone's phones."

"Oh, no! We want you in the picture too," the first girl said.

Rowan shook her head. "You don't even know who I am."

"You're Rowan," the second girl said matter-of-factly.

"Everyone who follows Luke Stone knows who you are. You're all anyone's talking about on his fan page."

"Oh…really?"

"O.M.G. Yes! It's *so* romantic, the way he stopped your wedding. Like something out of a movie."

"Fans are dying to know if you're together and here you are, doing normal people stuff."

"We are normal people," Luke said.

"But not like, normal normal people," the third girl said. "I mean, we're on a history class field trip. You're just like…here."

Luke managed to get them all in frame together—the girls grinning ear-to-ear and Rowan doing her best not to look like the awkward random person caught in the picture.

"Can you sign my notebook, too?" the second girl asked.

"Did you guys get married?" the first girl whispered to Rowan.

"No, sorry," she whispered back.

"Oh." She looked crestfallen. "I really wanted you guys to be married."

"Why?"

"Because that would be over-the-top romantic."

"You don't think it would be a little weird to be getting ready to marry one man one second and turn around and marry a different man the next?" Rowan asked.

"Maybe, but I just think it's super romantic."

"Yeah, you've said that," Rowan said. "A couple of times."

"I want someone to love me enough to barge into a wedding to stop it." She sighed and blinked puppy dog eyes at Luke.

Well, all right then.

"Luke, are you going to record that song you sang at the wedding?" the third girl asked.

"Yeah, we've tried to find it, but the only videos on YouTube are from the wedding and the song cuts off when Rowan walks away," the first girl said.

"There's a YouTube video?" Rowan asked.

"Oh, yeah. You guys have like a gajillion views."

Wonderful.

They finally extricated themselves from the group and left the plantation.

"Did you bring anything dressy? I can call and get us reservations for dinner," Luke said.

"I'm too tired to go out for dinner. Can we order in again? Maybe Thai?"

"Sure, we can do that."

Sitting on one of the tall stools in the kitchen, Rowan rested her elbow on the counter and propped her head on her fist while Luke called in their food order. It would be really great if he had a couch for her to curl up on. She looked at the small area next to the kitchen. A comfortable loveseat and wide chair would look really cute there. Add a rug, a couple of tables, and some plants and it would be the perfect place to relax while someone was cooking in the kitchen.

"So I'm thinking tomorrow we can go to Opryland Resort for lunch. It's a lot easier to get lunch reservations than dinner. We can do the General Jackson for dinner. Maybe not tomorrow, but the day after? I'll look up the schedule online and see what shows they have."

Just thinking about running all over town again made her tired. "Luke, stop."

"Stop what?"

"Stop treating me like I'm some out of town guest that you have to entertain."

"That's not what I'm doing," he said, turning away from her.

"It is," she said. "Either that or you don't want to spend any time alone with me."

He turned back toward her. "Of course, I want to be alone with you."

"Do you?" She was afraid to push him, but she was more afraid coming to Nashville had been a mistake. He'd been sweet and polite and gracious and all she could think was he was acting that way because he realized he'd made a mistake asking her there.

"Because we haven't talked. Not really. Not about this." She gestured between them. "Not about what's going on right now. I don't need you to show me everything I've missed. I need you to show me where we're supposed to go from here."

He braced his hands on the counter. "I'm trying, Rowan."

"Trying to what?" She heard the frustration in his voice, but she was just as frustrated.

"Trying to do the right thing. Trying to make up for my mistakes—past and present. I'm trying to not be the selfish asshole who drags you off to his bed."

A wave of heat rushed through her body before it pooled between her legs. "Maybe you should try being a selfish asshole, because being the apologetic good guy isn't working."

"You want me to be an asshole? I'll be an asshole." He took three large steps, gripped her head between his hands, and smashed his lips to hers.

Finally.

CHAPTER 24

She didn't pull away. He took that as a positive sign. It took a few seconds to register that she was actively kissing him back, tangling her tongue with his, and he groaned. He stepped closer and pushed his thigh between her legs.

Her arms wrapped around his waist and he felt her fist his shirt at his back.

He moved away from her mouth and trailed across her jawline to her neck. "God, Rowan. I've missed you so much."

"You haven't been lacking for company," she said.

He lifted his head to look in her eyes. "It wasn't the same. It was never the same. You are, and have always been, the only woman for me. The only person in the world who gets *me*."

Her eyes flitted between his as she searched his gaze. She pushed him back and his heart sank when she stood. "You know, it would be really convenient right now if you had a couch downstairs because your bedroom is a really long way away."

A wide grin took over his face. "I'll take you shopping tomorrow. You can pick out all the couches you want." Bending down, he hooked his arm behind her knees and lifted her, cradling her in his embrace as his legs ate up the distance between the kitchen and the stairs.

She wrapped her arms around his shoulders, tilted her head to kiss his neck, and giggled.

"What's so funny?"

"Last night I was thinking I wanted you to sweep me off my feet like Rhett Butler and carry me up to your bedroom."

He almost stumbled on the first step when she licked along his jawline and sucked on his ear. "Jesus."

"Don't trip," she said.

"Maybe you shouldn't do that while we're on the stairs," he replied.

Her mouth didn't leave his neck. "What should I do, then?" she said against his skin.

"Just hold on, Scarlett."

She smiled against his neck.

Concentrating on climbing the stairs, he cursed how many of them there were. He was slightly winded when he finally reached the landing of the second floor, but he didn't pause on his way to his room. There was no way in hell he was going to give Rowan a chance to rethink her decision—it had been hell keeping his hands away from her all day.

Although, with the way her fingers were clenched in his shirt, that might not be a worry.

Finally, his bed was in sight. Rather than tossing her onto it like some cheesy romantic comedy, he set her down at the side of it. He would give her a chance to run, if that was what she wanted.

He brushed a strand of hair away from her eyes. "Are you sure?"

"Yes," she said. "I'm sure."

Relief was sweet as it coursed through him. He hadn't been a monk, but he hadn't lied when he said it wasn't the same. There was always something missing. A piece that never fit quite right.

Rowan fit. In every way that mattered and he wanted to savor this moment.

He lowered his head as she raised hers until their lips fused. Gently. Now that she was here, he was in no rush.

She ran her hands up and down his chest until stopping at vee of his shirt. She slipped the buttons out of the holes, one-by-one until it hung open.

His stomach muscles clenched when her fingers touched his skin. He wished he'd gone to the gym more. He wasn't fat, but he'd lost some definition the last few months he'd been on the road. She'd always liked circling her fingers around his abs when they were together.

Rowan tugged at his belt buckle and he stopped her.

"What?" she asked.

"Let's leave my pants on for a little while longer. If I take them off now, I'm not going to be able to take my time."

"I'm okay with that."

"I'm not." He pushed her hands away and grabbed the hem of her shirt. "If you're in a rush to get someone naked, let's get you naked."

She grinned up at him and raised her hands above her head. "Okay."

He grinned back and peeled her shirt off, dropping it on the floor. The flesh-colored bra was simple but created a deep cleavage between her breasts and his mouth watered.

"If you're just going to stand there and stare, I might as well give you a show." She reached behind her back.

"No. Let me."

Goose bumps rose on her arms when he ran his hands around her back. He kissed the crook of her neck as he unhooked the fastening and she tilted her head to the side and sighed. He slid the straps down her arms and the garment fell.

Her breasts filled his hands when he cupped them and her nipples hardened against his palm. She'd always been so sensitive.

"Can we at least take your shirt off, too?" she asked.

"I suppose that's fair." He undid the buttons at the cuffs and peeled his shirt off, dropping it next to hers. The sight of her half naked in front of him made his knees buckle and he knelt in front of her.

"When did you get this?" He flicked the belly ring with his tongue.

"A few years ago." Her nails scraped across the back of his head, sending frissons of electricity down his spine.

From this angle, he could see a small black tattoo just under her left breast. He ran his thumb over the small swirl. "And this?"

Her fingers stilled. "A year after we broke up. It's the Celtic symbol for new beginnings."

He pressed his lips over the spot, then looked up at her. "This is our new beginning."

Standing, he picked her up again and laid her on the bed, following her down. Her dark amber eyes were shiny and he knew she was holding back tears. He didn't want her crying. Sighing, laughing, maybe screaming—but not crying.

He kissed his way down to her jeans and flicked the button open. Rising up on his knees, he pulled them down her legs and tossed them away, peeling her socks off as well.

Her hips were fuller. Her abdomen a little softer. She was more beautiful than he remembered. She'd blossomed and he'd missed it. Never again. This was their new beginning.

"I'd really like you to take your pants off as well," she said.

"I knew you just wanted to get me naked." He winked and sat up to pull off his boots, socks, and jeans, but kept his boxer briefs on.

She surprised him by straddling him and settling right over his very hard erection.

"Row," he said with a groan.

Grabbing his head, she kissed him while moving back and

forth, up and down. Her damp heat surrounded him and gripped her hips while groaning into her mouth.

He let her take the lead until his balls felt like they were going to explode. Damned if he'd blow his load in his shorts like it was their first time again.

"Stand up," he said.

Using his shoulders for balance, she stood and he pulled her panties down her hips and legs, helping her step out of them.

She'd waxed. Almost completely bare.

"Fuck." His dick throbbed at the sight. Leaning forward he tasted her, drawing a deep groan.

"Luke," she whispered. "Oh god, that feels good."

He rubbed and flicked at her clit, circling it with the tip of his tongue once then with the wide part, alternating back and forth.

"Luke." Her voice held a little more desperation and he knew she was close.

Selfishly, he didn't want her to come without him. Not this first time back together. He eased off and ran a hand down the back of her leg, putting pressure behind her knee to get her to straddle him again.

"Can we get you fully naked now?" she asked.

He grinned. "Yeah. If you dig around in the top drawer of the nightstand on your left, you should find some condoms.

While she searched for a condom, he lay back to pull off his underwear. With her half straddling him, half leaning on the edge of the bed, it was like the worst game of Twister he'd ever played.

Her breast pressed against his face when she straightened up. Or best.

"You only have two."

He took a blue foil square from her. "I guess we better make them count then."

Ripping open the packet, he rolled the condom down. Rowan played with his balls and he fought to sheath himself quickly.

Finally ready, he gripped her hips again and positioned her over him.

She gripped him gently and guided him where she needed him. Hissing through his clenched teeth, he watched as she slowly slid down his cock until he was balls deep and finally complete.

Pushing up, he bent his knees a little and sat up so they were chest to chest. This position wouldn't give either of them a lot of leverage, but he wanted to be close—as close as he could get.

He rested his forehead against hers. "You good?" he asked.

"Yes," she whispered. She swiveled her hips.

It was a gentle movement, but she might as well have yanked on his dick. He threaded his fingers through the hair at the nape of her neck, pulling her mouth to his. He mimicked the movement of her hips with his tongue, swirling around hers.

He hadn't been wrong. He wasn't going to last long at all. The tension was building again as his sac grew tight and he tried to stem the relief he knew was close. The more he tried to hold off, the more it seemed futile.

Sweat slicked their bodies and trickled down his back. Wedging his hand between them, he found her clit and she moaned into his mouth, the pace of her hips increasing. She broke the kiss and panted against his mouth.

"I can tell you're close," he said in a low voice. "I can feel your muscles around me as you move, squeezing me tight."

"Oh my god."

"I want to come so bad, but I want to feel you come around me first. I want you to squeeze me so tight inside you it'll feel like you'll never let me go." He rubbed faster, pressing hard when she rolled her hips against his.

Her breath caught in the back of her throat and her head fell back as her core clenched tight around him. That was all he needed and he let go. The relief was instantaneous and he pulled her down onto him, thrusting his hips up as she ground down onto him.

There was absolutely no space between them and yet he wanted her to be even closer.

Rowan's head dropped to his shoulder as she came down from her high. His body still shuddered with the aftereffects of his orgasm. Still holding her tight, he fell back on the bed and she adjusted to tuck her head into space under his chin.

"You okay?" he asked.

She cleared her throat. "I don't know. Ask me again in a few minutes."

Male satisfaction surged through him and he smirked. Never mind he wasn't sure whether his legs would work or not when he tried to get up to get rid of the condom.

"Do you want to shower before we go to sleep?" he asked.

"That sounds nice," she whispered.

He chuckled and rolled to the side, reaching between them to keep the condom in place as he slid out of her. "Let's do that before you fall asleep, then."

She groaned, but sat up and rubbed her eyes. "A quick one."

He kissed her. "Promise."

CHAPTER 25

Rowan inhaled deeply and stretched under the weight of Luke's arm around her waist. For the first time in weeks, she didn't wake up dreading the day or what was in front of her. But she couldn't help but wonder what last night had meant. She didn't regret sleeping with him, but at the same time, she still had so many doubts about what lay ahead for them and what it meant for their future.

His arm tightened around her and he burrowed his face in the crook of his neck. "What are you thinking about so hard this early in the morning?"

"It's almost ten," she said.

"Still too early to be thinking that hard. What are you worrying about?"

She turned toward him. His eyes were still closed. "How do you know I'm worrying?"

"Because I know you and it's what you do." He shifted to his side and propped his head on one hand. "What's up?"

"I'm just—What does it say about me that two weeks ago I was ready to marry someone else and now I'm in bed with you?"

His brow furrowed as he frowned. "Nothing. It says absolutely nothing about you. It says I finally broke through and was able to convince you that I'm serious about us, because I know you wouldn't have had sex with me if you weren't sure about that."

"You wouldn't say that if you'd read some of the comments on social media."

"Shit." He rolled on his back and pulled her to his side. "I quit reading anything written about me on social media a long time ago. Those people are assholes."

"Is it how you thought it would be?" she asked. "Being a famous country music singer?"

"Some of it. When I'm in the studio making music or I'm singing in front of a crowd...it's the best feeling in the world. That's what I thought it would be like. But the other stuff...the public appearances and the social media trolls and the critics— that crap I could do without, but it's all part of the package. I can't have one without the other."

"Would you change anything, if you could?"

He tilted his head to look at her. "Just one thing. You?"

"Just one thing," she whispered.

"We can't go back and change things." He kissed her forehead. "We can only go forward and try not to make the same mistakes we did before."

They lay there for several minutes. Rowan closed her eyes and was on the edge of falling back asleep when Luke asked, "What made you change your mind?"

"About what?"

"Coming out here."

"Michael."

"What about him?" She could hear his disgruntlement.

"He came by the apartment and we talked about what happened."

"How'd that go?"

She shrugged. "It was fine. I think we realized we'd both been having doubts about getting married for a while, but neither of us wanted to hurt the other. We weren't in love with each other anymore. He asked about you and I told him you wanted me to come here. He said I should do it. Not because *you* deserved another chance, but because I did."

She tilted her head back to look at him.

"Hmm. I'll have to send him a thank you card."

She smiled and snuggled back into the crook of his shoulder.

"How long are you staying?" he asked.

"I don't know."

He shifted under her. "What do you mean you don't know?"

"I bought an open-ended ticket," she said. "I didn't want to come out here with a timer counting down in the back of my mind. I wanted to see how things went without any external pressure."

He rolled over her and settled between her legs. "So you could stay forever."

"I have a job and an apartment in Colorado." She ran her hands on the outside of his upper arms.

"You could have a job here and you already have a house," he said with a smirk.

"*If* I moved back here, I would want my own place to begin with."

"No. *When* you move back here, you're moving in with me. This is it—you and me. It always has been and I'm not wasting any more time pretending otherwise."

A surge of adrenaline coursed through her veins.

"What if I want to stay in Denver?" she asked.

"Then I'll move to Denver."

She cocked her head. "You'd do that?"

"Rowan, you're not getting it. I will do whatever it takes if it means we're together—I thought I had already proved that."

Her heart thudded in her chest and she teetered on a precipice. She'd known when she made the decision to come out here that this moment would happen. This or they would figure out they shouldn't be together. But she hadn't really prepared herself for either. Fear was a powerful thing and her fear of being hurt again was as great as her fear of never having Luke in her life again.

The question was—which possibility was worse? *'Tis better to have loved and lost, than never to have loved at all.*

"Okay," she said.

A wide, slow smile split his face. "Okay? Really?"

"Yes. We need to talk about some things. I really like Colorado and I'm not sure I want to move back to Tennessee, so if you weren't serious about that say something now so I can resign myself to the idea, but I want to be with you."

His kiss was hard. "That's all I want. I like Colorado. I can record anywhere. I might have to find a new band, but if I can convince the label to pay for their moving expenses some of them might be willing to move. Or I can come here to record. I can afford to fly back and forth. We can keep this house and buy another one in Colorado, maybe not as big though."

She laughed. "Luke, slow down. We don't have to figure everything out right this minute. We have time."

"Thank you. Thank you. Thank you." He peppered her cheeks with kisses between each *thank you.* "I thought I was going to have to tickle you into agreeing with me."

"That's not even funny," she said.

"What? You don't like being tickled?"

She jerked when his fingers found the sensitive spot between her ribs. "Don't, Luke. I'm not kidding."

"Don't what?" He got her again.

That was it. He seemed to have forgotten she knew his spots, too. Reaching between them, she dug her thumb into his hip joint at the top of his thigh.

"Whoa! Hey now." He tried to get away.

"What?" she asked. "Something wrong?"

"Okay, you're right. No tickle torture."

"That's what I thought," she said.

"For me!" He grabbed her hands in one of his and tickled her ribs with the other.

She shrieked and tried to wriggle away, kicking and squirming. Her legs became tangled in the sheets, limiting her range of motion. She got one of her hands free and jabbed him in the hip, forcing him to retreat. They wrestled around on the bed, laughing and yelling.

"Luke!" A woman's voice rang out, followed by a sharp whistle.

Rowan gasped and scrambled to cover her exposed body.

Luke did the same thing. "Marla. What are you doing here? How did you get in?"

Who the hell was Marla?

"I used my key. You weren't answering your phone." She stood in the doorway, one hand over her eyes. "Is it safe to look now?"

Why the hell did she have a key?

"Yes," Luke said as he adjusted the sheet around his hip.

She peeked through her fingers before lowering her hand. "You forgot, didn't you?" Whoever she was, she sighed the sigh of a woman used to being put out.

"About what?"

"The gala in two days? Your sister will be here in the morning." She tapped at the tablet in the crook of her arm. "Your tux is at the cleaners—I'm picking it up later today. Shelby has a dress fitting at ten tomorrow—I'll update the appointment to include Rowan."

She looked up from her tablet. "You are going to be here on Saturday, right?" She didn't give Rowan a chance to answer. "There shouldn't be a problem getting you a ticket…the seating arrangement might need some adjustment. I'll have to talk to Lisa about that."

Rowan thought she might have been talking to herself out loud at that point.

"I'll be here at nine-fifteen tomorrow to pick you up, Rowan. What kind of coffee do you like?"

"Uh…regular. With cream. I can fix some here."

"Perfect." She lowered the tablet. "It's very nice to meet you, Rowan. I'll see you tomorrow."

Frowning as the woman disappeared, Rowan looked at Luke. "What just happened?"

"Marla." He sighed and flopped back on the bed.

"And she is…?"

"My new PR slash PA. The woman's a powerhouse. I'm pretty sure that tablet is physically attached to her arm."

"What happened to Joe Bob?"

"Bobby John? He retired."

She tilted her head. "Huh. Where am I going Saturday?"

He grinned. "Wanna go to a party with me? It's for a good cause."

CHAPTER 26

"You're really here!" Shelby launched herself out of the car and hugged Rowan.

Rowan hugged her back. In many ways, Shelby had been closer than Adalynn. The backs of her eyes stung as the realization she'd lost more than Luke when they'd broken up hit her hard.

"I missed you too, Shelby," she said.

Shelby pushed her away. "Whose fault is that?"

"Touché."

"I don't care if my brother screws this up again—"

"Hey! I can hear you," Luke said, joining them and wrapping his arm around Rowan's shoulders.

Shelby glared at him. "If he screws up again, I get to keep you."

Rowan smiled. "Deal."

"Good. Now, he promised to pay for my dress if I went to the gala thingy and this is probably the only time I'm ever going to be able to walk a red carpet, so if he can't take us both, he's going to have to stay home and we'll go together."

"I'm right here," he said. "Could you stop talking about me as if I'm not?"

"No," Shelby said. "But I'll leave the important stuff for when you're not with us."

Marla came through the front door. "Okay, let's get a move on. Our appointment is in forty-five minutes and it's going to take at least thirty to get there."

Luke pulled Rowan closer and wrapped his arms loosely around her waist. Leaning close to her ear, he whispered, "If they get too nosy, call me and I'll rescue you."

"I think I'll be okay," she said.

"Call me anyway." He clasped her jaw and kissed her.

She pressed closer as their tongues caressed each other. How badly did she really need a dress?

The clearing of a throat split them apart. Shelby stared at them, grinning like a crazy person while Marla looked pointedly at her watch. She was probably the one who cleared her throat.

"All right," Luke said. "Have fun." He followed them out the front door and waved as they drove off.

Shelby leaned between the front seats. "On a scale of one to set everything on fire, how mad were you at Luke when he objected at your wedding?"

One thing she'd always loved about Shelby was her willingness to lay it all out there. "He didn't actually object. We'd decided to leave that part out since we hadn't seen the point."

Shelby laughed. "Oh, the irony." Her laughter trailed off. "Sorry I didn't RSVP, but going felt kind of like a betrayal to Luke. I was happy for you, but at the same time, it didn't seem right. You know?"

She did. "I debated whether or not to send you and your mama an invitation, but in the end, it felt more wrong not to. I didn't get an RSVP from your mom either, not that I was really expecting one. Although, I didn't know she moved to Johnson City, so she might not have ever received it."

"Luke surprised her with a house. He bought it with his first big royalty check."

Buying houses for the women in his life seemed to be a thing. "That was sweet of him."

"It really was. And it's a cute house, too. He paid off all my student loans and paid for graduate school."

"What's your degree in?" Rowan asked.

"Early childhood education. I started out as a teacher, but I love working with kids that need a little extra attention so I ended up transferring to the special needs program."

"That's so impressive. I don't think I would have the patience to teach kids."

"I love it. Kids are honest—what you see is what you get. Your mama said you finished dental school."

Rowan's eyebrows rose. "You guys still talk?"

"We run into each other every now and then. She seems really proud of the fact that you're a doctor."

Hmm. She'd never said as much to her. "It's not like I'm curing cancer—I fix peoples' teeth."

"It still makes you a doctor."

A ringing noise sounded through the car's speakers. "La Privé."

"Hi, Gloria. This is Marla. We're about five minutes away."

"I'll send Adam out to wait for you."

"Thank you. See you soon." Marla pressed a button on the steering wheel and disconnected the call.

She glanced at Rowan. "Parking is a pain in the ass this time of day, so they block off one of the spots whenever I make an appointment."

"Wow, that's service," Shelby said.

"For as much as we're going to spend, it's the least they do."

Rowan's cheeks flushed. "Uh…Marla, not to be crass but I don't have a lot of money to spend on a dress. I wasn't planning on spending more than a couple hundred dollars."

Marla smiled. "Oh, you're not spending a dime—Luke is."

"I'm not really comfortable with that," she said.

"Too late," Marla said. "He called ahead with his credit card information and gave me explicit instructs to spare no expense, so I don't plan to. It's the least *he* can do after what he's put you through."

"Amen, sister," Shelby said from the back.

Apparently, Marla was on Team Rowan. She turned left at the next light and stopped half-way down the block and waved at a man in a suit standing in front of a parking spot.

He leaned forward, glanced through the windshield, then smiled and stepped out of the way when he saw Marla.

She parallel parked on the first try, earning a decent amount of awe from Rowan. It always took her at least three tries when she had to do it.

Her door was opened as soon as Marla shut off the engine and the man offered a hand to assist her out. She managed not to clothesline herself with the seatbelt and made what she thought was a semi-graceful exit.

"Thank you, Adam," Marla said.

"Of course. Gloria is waiting for you upstairs." He jogged ahead of them to open the door to the nondescript storefront and they followed Marla in.

Rowan clenched her teeth to keep from gaping. The color scheme was beige and muted bronze with plush couches and glass tables.

Shelby slipped her hand into Rowan's and squeezed. "I dare you to ask one of the employees if they work on commission," she whispered.

Rowan stared at her for a heartbeat and snorted out a giggle. "I thought it was just me."

"Oh, no." Shelby shook her head. "I feel like Julia Roberts following Richard Gere into the store. All that's missing is the hooker dress and thigh-high boots."

"How much money do you think we're going to spend?" Rowan asked in a low voice.

Marla stopped in front of a curtain and pulled it back,

revealing a flight of stairs. "Not quite obscene, but we're definitely going to do some damage."

She gestured for them to go up and then followed them, drawing the curtain closed behind them.

~

ROWAN'S HEAD lolled back against the chair as the pedicurist rubbed her feet.

"Is this normal?" she asked.

"If it is, I need to marry someone famous," Shelby said.

"For something like the Academy of Country Music awards, yes," Marla said. "For a fundraising gala, not usually. But Luke said to make sure you both received the VVIP treatment."

"VVIP?" Shelby asked.

"Very, *very* important person," Marla explained.

"Oh. In that case, I definitely need to marry someone famous. Do you know anyone?"

Marla smiled wryly. "Matchmaking isn't usually something I put on my resume, but I'll see what I can do."

"Excellent." Shelby sipped the sparkling wine they'd been provided as soon as they'd sat down.

Almost four hours later, they'd been pampered, poked, and fitted for exquisite dresses that would be delivered to Luke's the next day in plenty of time for them to be pampered again by a hairdresser and professional make-up artist and make it to the gala.

"Can I see your phone for a second?" Marla asked as they waited for Shelby to return from the restroom.

"Why?" Rowan asked.

"I want to program my number in it."

"Oh. Sure." She unlocked her phone and handed it over.

Thumbs flying across the screen, Marla said, "Don't hesitate to call if you need anything."

Rowan took her phone back. "I think you've covered just about everything. I can't think of a single thing I would need for tomorrow."

"Not just tomorrow. For anything." She crossed her arms, seeming not to know what to do with her empty hands. "Look, I get paid a lot of money to keep track of Luke. He's a pain in the ass sometimes because he doesn't care about all the publicity stuff that goes along with his job and that makes *my* job harder. But he's also one of the most down-to-earth honest people I've ever met in this industry and I genuinely like him. I—"

"What?" Rowan asked when she didn't continue.

"Well…other than when he's on stage or in a recording booth, I think this morning is the first time I've seen him truly happy. I think you're the reason for that. I know a little bit about what happened before and I want you to know I'm an ally and I hope eventually a friend. So if you ever need anything, please call me."

Rowan searched Marla's earnest gaze and found nothing but sincerity. "Thank you. I feel like I've been on an emotional roller-coaster since my almost wedding. I think things are finally settling down, but at the same time there's a lot of unknown ahead."

"I'm only a phone call away." Marla rubbed her shoulder.

"Thank you. It'll be nice having a friendly face out here."

CHAPTER 27

"Ready?" Luke asked as they pulled up to the front of the Parthenon. He should have remembered the gala was going to be here—he could have taken Rowan somewhere else the other afternoon instead.

"Yes," Shelby said. "Is someone walking us in while you take pictures?

"Shell—you're walking in with me."

"Wait—what?" Rowan asked.

"Yes!" Shelby pumped a fist in the air.

Luke took Rowan's hand and wrapped it in his. The color had drained from her face. "Marla didn't explain how tonight would go?"

She shook her head, eyes wide. "No. I just assumed you'd do the press thing while we—I—went inside to wait for you."

"You can if you want." He leaned closer. "I'd really like to walk in holding your hand though."

This was the first chance he had to introduce her to the world as his. He knew the reporters were going to go nuts when they saw him and Rowan together—he'd talked to Marla about it—but one, it would hopefully help kill any rumors going around and two, he wanted there to be no doubt that they were together.

Rowan swallowed visibly but nodded.

"Thank you. I'll be right by you the whole time."

"Me, too," Shelby said.

The limo stopped and the door opened, an usher waiting for them to exit. He knew these things were timed to the second, so he levered himself out of the car. Reaching in, he helped Shelby out first—he didn't want to have to let go of Rowan once he had her hand.

Camera flashes, already popping, went crazy as soon as he pulled her out. A man with a headset, microphone, and tablet gestured for them to move forward and join the line of other people arriving.

"Jeez. This is like a ride at Disney World," Rowan said.

"I don't know…I think Disney could use some pointers on efficiency. It's like a small army running things," Shelby said.

Watching their awe, Luke remembered his first big event and how out of place he'd felt. This wasn't even a big industry show—just a local fundraiser. He still felt like an imposter. Any minute now, someone would come rip off his Stetson and demand he leave.

"Is that the governor?" Shelby asked.

Luke looked around the couple in front of them. "I think so."

"How tacky would it be if I started asking for autographs?" she asked.

"I don't know. Are you going to ask them to sign your boobs?" Rowan asked.

Shelby grinned. "A couple of them maybe."

"Mr. Stone, you're next," one of the ushers said.

"I've got them," Marla said, joining them. "Sorry I'm late. There was an issue with Laney's dress."

"Laney Faith?" Shelby asked. "I love her!"

"Good. You're sitting next to her at dinner. Just please don't mention anything about how short her skirt is—she's already self-conscience about it."

"Of course not," Shelby said.

"Rowan, Shelby, if you look at the carpet, there are tape 'X's. That's where you'll stop so the press can take pictures and ask questions."

Luke squeezed Rowan's hand. "No one told me that little tidbit my first event. I just walked straight through. Never even paused except to tap a couple people on the shoulder to say excuse me."

Rowan grinned and laughed, which was exactly what he hoped to achieve. He didn't want her worrying about anything.

"All right. You're up in thirty seconds," Marla said. "Don't answer any personal questions and just keep smiling."

Rowan's smile slipped and Luke leaned forward to whisper, "Are you wearing any underwear? 'Cause I'm not."

"Go." Marla gave him a small push on the back of his arm.

He winked at Rowan and led them down the gauntlet.

OF COURSE EVERYONE shouted questions about their relationship. He gave the answers he and Marla had discussed—basically that it was a private matter they were working on privately. Once inside, Marla peeled off to check on Laney since she was presenting, and they were led to their table.

"Anyone want a drink?" he asked.

"Please, god, yes," Rowan said.

He kissed her cheek. "I love hearing those words come out of your mouth," he whispered.

Her eyes widened and her cheeks took on a deep blush.

"Shush!" She smacked his shoulder while he laughed.

"Would you two get a room?" Shelby asked.

"We will just as soon as this thing is over," he said.

"How long is this going to last?" Shelby asked.

"It'll be around two hours before we can gracefully exit. You're welcome to stay if you want."

"Maybe. We'll see how the night goes."

"Do you want wine or something stronger," he asked Rowan.

"Wine," she said. "A semi-sweet white, please."

"Coming right up." He kissed her gently. "Shell, you want a beer?"

"Hell, no. I want champagne. We're fancy tonight."

Luke chuckled. "Fancy it is. I'll be right back." Kissing Rowan again, he squeezed her and headed to the bar.

"Hey, man. You avoiding me?' Brett leaned against the bar. Outwardly, he looked relaxed, but Luke could see tension around his eyes and mouth.

"Hey. Just been busy." He didn't want to get into it with Brett at the gala and more and more lately all they seemed to do was argue about the direction Luke wanted to take with his career.

"With Rowan," Brett said.

The way he said it, the tone in his voice, made the hair on the back of Luke's neck stand on end.

"Yeah. And my mom and sister. You know—family."

"Whatever." Brett gestured to the bartender and ordered a scotch, neat. "The label wants you back in the studio. They're getting antsy that you haven't signed the new contract. They're worried someone else is trying to poach you."

Luke watched Brett down half his glass in one gulp. "I know. I've got a meeting with Walter on Monday."

Brett set down his glass with a thud. "What do you mean you have a meeting with Walter? Since when?"

"Since his secretary called and asked if I was available to go over the contract. I assumed you'd set it up." He took the stemmed glasses and long-neck the bartender gave him. "Look, I'm gonna head back to the table. If I don't see you before the end of the night, I'll call you on Monday."

Weaving through the crowd, he saw Laney had joined them at the table.

"Ladies." He handed Rowan and Shelby their glasses and slipped his arm around Rowan's waist. "Laney, can I get you something?"

"Oh, no, thank you." She rested her hands over her stomach and laughed. "I never drink at these things—I get nervous enough as it is."

Rowan tilted her head up to him. "Do you still get nervous?"

"I still get butterflies. Especially at things like this. It's different than being on stage singing."

"Exactly," Laney said. "It's different during a concert because you've rehearsed so often it's a routine, but I've only had one walk-through for this. Plus, the zipper on my dress broke and I had to switch to my back up and now I feel like everyone can see my panties."

Luke studiously looked everywhere except the hem of Laney's dress.

"No," Shelby said. "It's nowhere near that short. I think it's perfectly fine."

"Really?" Laney asked. "You're not just saying that?"

"I promise."

A bell chimed and a man in a tuxedo stepped up to the podium. "Ladies and gentlemen, if you'll kindly take your seats dinner will be served. The presentation portion of the evening will begin between the dinner service and dessert."

The hall filled with the sound of rustling clothes and the clink of silverware as everyone sat down. Twenty minutes into dinner, Luke's phone vibrated in his pocket and he pulled it out, checking the screen.

He leaned across Rowan to catch Shelby and Laney's attention. "Laney, Marla said they need you backstage."

She jolted in her seat. "Oh! Shoot! Do you mind walking me back there? I feel so self-conscious going by myself."

Luke glanced at Rowan. "Will you be okay if I walk her back?"

Rowan grinned. "I'm a big girl. I think I'll be okay for a few minutes."

"And I'm here," Shelby chimed in. "I'll beat up anyone that bothers her."

He rolled his eyes and kissed Rowan quickly. "I'll be back soon." He pushed away from the table and walked around Rowan and Shelby to where Laney waited nervously for him.

He should tell her, but they'd had such a good night and if he told her she'd leave—he knew it in the bottom of his soul, with no doubt. She wouldn't understand. Hell, she probably wouldn't even give him a chance to explain and he couldn't really blame her. No matter how he tried to think of a way to explain, it didn't sound good. No one had been around when it happened and he knew Laney would never say anything. Rowan never had to know.

"You're awfully quiet," Rowan said.

He reached for her hand and smiled. "Just tired."

Shelby's jaw cracked as she yawned. "No kidding. You can keep being rich and famous if it's always so exhausting."

"Not always. Award season is crazy, but that's usually it."

"Shelby, when are you going back?" Rowan asked.

"Wednesday morning. I'm going to meet up with some college friends tomorrow and Monday. You're welcome to tag along with me if you get tired of hanging out with Luke."

"That's not a bad idea, actually. I need to go in for a meeting on Monday," Luke said.

"I was going to call the clinic Monday and tell my boss I need more time off," Rowan said.

A wide grin took over his face and he slid his hand behind her neck. "How much time off?"

"I thought I'd start with a month," she said.

"I can work with a month." He leaned across the space between them to kiss her. Her lips were soft and tasted faintly of the wine she'd drunk at the dinner.

She rested her hand on his cheek. "I want to give this a chance to work. That's going to take more than a week."

"Thank you," he whispered.

"Awesome. We're home," Shelby said with a yawn.

Rowan pulled away and grinned.

"If you two are going to stay in the car and make googly eyes at each other all night, can I have the keys to the house, please?" Shelby wiggled her fingers.

"We're getting out," Luke said.

Shelby opened the door to the car he'd hired and Rowan followed her out. Luke thanked the driver and handed him a hundred-dollar bill as a tip, then climbed out after the women, taking Rowan's hand as they walked to the door. It felt so normal —so right—coming home with her. Something he could see doing for the rest of his life.

Once inside, he tossed his keys and caught them. "It would be useful having a table in here to put things on."

"Among other things," Rowan said.

"We can go shopping tomorrow," he said.

On the upstairs landing, Shelby headed to the guest bedroom Rowan was in originally. "Try to keep the crazy monkey sex noises down to a minimum."

Luke shook his head and steered Rowan toward his bedroom. There was enough space between the bedrooms that there was no way Shelby would be able to hear them. Just in case, he made sure to close the door tight.

Rowan kicked off her heels and sighed. "Are you sure you're okay? You've been weird since you came back to the table after you went backstage."

He stepped close and grasped her head. Time for the truth. The truth that mattered more than anything else.

"I love you, Rowan. I've loved you since we were sixteen years old and you sucker punched Matt Chester after he beaned me in the head with that pitch during practice because I asked you to spring formal first."

She placed her hands over his. "Is that why he did it? All I knew was he'd hurt my best friend."

"You're more than that. You are the woman I want to spend the rest of my life with. You're the one I want to wake up next to. The one I want to have a family with. And the one who will tell me you love my music when I think it sucks. I will do anything and everything to make you believe that."

She was quiet for several seconds and sweat trickled down the middle of his back.

She placed a hand over his heart, slipping under the lapel of his jacket. "I believe it." She pushed on his chest and backed him toward the bed, a sexy smile teasing her lips.

It might not be the three words he was hoping for, but they would do for now.

CHAPTER 28

"How extended of an absence are you talking about?" Joyce, Rowan's boss, asked.

"I'm not sure. At least a month." Rowan flipped the pen in her hand end over end, tapping it on the counter.

"Are you moving to Nashville?" Joyce asked.

She took a deep breath. "I'm not sure, but it's a serious possibility."

"What are you sure about?"

Wasn't that the question. Luke said he loved her and she hadn't said it in return. It had been on the tip of her tongue, but something had held her back. Some sense of self-preservation kept her from telling Luke she loved him. She did—to the depths of her soul—but it hadn't felt right for her to say it in that moment. Maybe it was because she wanted to say it without being prompted.

Maybe she didn't know what the hell she was doing and was grasping at straws. "Honestly? Not a lot."

"I can't keep your position vacant forever," Joyce said.

"I know."

Her sigh was heavy over the phone. "Two weeks. I need you to let me know one way or another in two weeks. If I don't hear from you by then, I'll take that as your resignation."

That would have to do. A month was a stretch anyway. "Thank you, Joyce."

"You're welcome. I hope it works out for you."

"Me, too."

She ended the conversation with another promise to call in the next two weeks. If she didn't know by then, she never would.

Out of morbid curiosity, she opened up her Facebook app and scrolled through her timeline. Her mentions were out of control, even after locking down her profile and weeding through her friends list.

Marla might have some tips on how to control that. Or Rowan might have to whittle her contacts down to close friends and family.

The phone pinged and buzzed at the same time a text bubble popped up.

> Should be done by 1. Wanna meet me for lunch?

A smile tugged at the corners of her mouth. He had tried to talk her into going with him that morning, but she'd wanted some alone time.

The doorbell chimed as she typed her response and she sent the reply before she answered the door.

> Waiting for the furniture, remember?

It was a little early for the delivery truck. The store had promised between twelve and two and it was just after eleven forty-five. No delivery she'd scheduled had ever been early—even if it was the first delivery of the day.

A weird sense of dread settled heavy in her stomach when she opened the door.

"Brett. Luke isn't here. He's at the label for a meeting."

He slapped the folder he held against his high. "I know. I'm here to see you, actually."

"Why?" She didn't care if she sounded like a bitch—Brett was not her favorite person and she wasn't going to expend the energy faking it.

"Can we talk inside?" He gestured behind her to the house.

Pressing her lips into a thin line, she stepped back and opened the door. A normal person would have waited in the foyer for the host to take the lead, but not Brett. No. He walked through to the kitchen, expecting her to follow.

"Asshole," she mumbled as she shut the door.

In the kitchen, she leaned against the counter and crossed her arms while he sat at the bar, spinning the folder on the counter a few times. He tapped it, then pushed it toward her.

"What?" She'd be damned if she made this easy for him. Whatever this was.

"You need to take a look at what's in there," he said in a low voice.

"Why?"

He looked at her from under his brow, a sympathetic look on his face. "Because if you're going to get involved with Luke again, I think you should go in fully informed."

"What does that mean?" she asked.

"He's not the same guy you knew in college, Rowan."

She glared at the folder, at Brett, and back at the folder. He made it sound like Luke had some dirty secret he was hiding.

She should tell him to get the hell out and take whatever it was with him. Instead, she inched toward it and gingerly opened it.

Her breath caught on a gasp.

Five pictures, in full Technicolor detail, of Luke. Kissing Laney Faith.

Laney's hand gripped the back of his head and Luke's hands rested on her hips.

"Where did these come from?"

"One of my friends is a photographer. We have a deal when it comes to pictures of my clients. He comes to me before releasing them when they might be…compromising."

She recognized Laney's outfit—the short skirt. These pictures were taken the night of the gala.

Luke had been uptight and nervous after he returned to their table from backstage. Later that night, he'd told her he loved her and she'd chalked it up to that.

"He loves you, Rowan," Brett said. "A blind man can see that. But some men aren't wired to be monogamous. I just wouldn't feel right if you went into a new relationship with him thinking you were the only one."

Nausea rolled in her stomach and she squeezed her eyes closed. "Get out."

"Rowan—"

"Get. Out," she said through gritted teeth.

She heard his clothes rustle. "For what it's worth…I'm sorry."

The front door opened and closed a few moments later. Her lip trembled and fat, hot tears rolled down her cheeks.

This.

This was exactly what she'd been afraid of. Now she understood what Michael had been talking about. She couldn't give her whole heart to Luke knowing she only had a piece of his—no matter how big of a piece it was. Coming second to his music was one thing, but she wouldn't compete with anyone else. She wouldn't do it six years ago when they were in college and she sure as hell wouldn't do it now.

Luke loved her—Brett was right about that and she knew it—but she had to be the only one in his life.

Leaving the pictures on the counter, she pushed away and went upstairs. She couldn't be there when he got home.

~

Luke pushed through the door, juggling the bags of food. "I hope you're good with barbecue," he called out. "I tried to call but your phone was off."

Shelby, not Rowan, sat at the kitchen counter.

He set the bags down and picked up the bottle of Johnny Walker Blue Label. It wasn't like his sister to hit the hard stuff.

"Kind of early for whisky, isn't it? Something happen?"

She took the bottle and silently poured three fingers into a glass and set it in front of him, then pushed a manila folder toward him.

"What's this?" he asked suspiciously.

Shelby gave him a baleful stare. "You tell me." She tipped the glass to her lips.

Luke flipped the folder open without breaking eye contact. Looking down a dull, heavy weight dug into his chest. Bracing his hands on the edge of the counter, he bent at the waist and hung his head between his arms.

Fuck!

Rising, he spread the photos out. Whoever took them had caught him in that moment of surprise before he'd managed to push Laney away.

"Where did these come from?"

"No idea. They were on the counter when I got back."

He shook his head. "Shelby, this isn't what it looks like."

"I know you, big brother. So I know it probably isn't. But no woman is going to see this and think it isn't exactly what it looks like," she said.

It sunk in that Rowan hadn't answered when he called. Shit.

"Rowan?" he shouted. He spun and raced upstairs, taking the steps two at a time. No sign of her in the bedroom and her clothes were gone, along with her suitcase.

Pulling his phone from his back pocket, he called her. It went directly to voice mail, as it had earlier. Rushing back downstairs, he tried again.

"Rowan—call me back, please. I promise it's not what it looks like. I swear to god, I would not cheat on you and there is nothing going on between me and Laney. Please call me back so I can explain. Please."

Reentering the kitchen, he flipped the photos over, looking for any indication of where they came from. The folder was plain. Nothing had any markings on it.

"Was she here when you got home?" he asked.

Shelby shook her head. "I would have tried to keep her here if she had been."

"Damn it! What time did you get back?"

"A little after one. I was going to see if she wanted lunch."

"All right. She texted me before noon, so a little more than an hour." He grabbed his hair, fisting while he paced. "Fuck. Why didn't I get the security cameras?"

"You don't have security cameras?"

"I didn't see the point." A thought occurred to him. "Is the furniture here?"

"They showed up about ten minutes after I did. Does it matter?"

"No. I was hoping if they had been here earlier, they might have seen whoever it was that brought the pictures. Fuck!"

He didn't know what to do. How was he supposed to find her and explain? Would she have gone back to Denver? Was she holed up in a hotel?

Marla. Marla would know how to find her. Snatching up his phone, he impatiently waited for her to answer.

"Hey, Luke. Can I call you back? I'm in the middle of something," she said.

"I'm sorry, Marla. I can't. I need you to find out if Rowan booked a flight home or maybe rented a car or checked into a hotel? I don't know…check the buses and trains as well."

"Why?" she asked.

"Someone delivered some pictures today and, taken out of context, they're bad. She took off and her phone is off."

"All right. I'll call you back."

"Please, Marla. I really need help with this."

"I know, Luke, but I need to make some calls. I'll let you know if I find something out, okay?"

"Okay." He ended the call and looked at Shelby. What choice did he have?

CHAPTER 29

*R*owan sipped her tea and stared unseeing at the tree covered hillside behind her parents' house. It reminded her a lot of the cabin in Colorado. Except she didn't have to start a generator in order to have a hot shower.

After calling an Uber to take her to the closest car rental place, she'd called her dad to see if she could visit for a few days. He was in Knoxville for a teacher's conference and her mom had tagged along. Rowan was disappointed and, at the same time, relieved she didn't have to listen to her mother's lamentations about everything going wrong in Rowan's life.

She was well aware, thank you very much. So there she was in Flat Holler, Tennessee. Where the most exciting thing to do on a Friday night was hang out in the parking lot of the Piggly Wiggly and go cow tipping. At least now there was a movie theater.

How did life get so complicated?

"So, what are you running from this time?"

Rowan jumped and sloshed hot tea on her shirt. "Sugar!"

She glared at Adalynn climbing the steps to the porch and pulled the material away from her chest.

"Sorry." Adalynn sat in the chair on the other side of the small table. "I thought you saw me."

"No. I was spacing. What are you doing here?"

"Mama said you were hiding out but wouldn't say why and asked me to check on you."

"I'm not hiding out. Or running." And even if she was, it was none of Adalynn's business.

"Sure you are." She picked up a handful of pretzels from the bowl on the table. "It's what you do. Things get hard, you quit, and you run. It's what you always do."

"No, it's not," she said through clenched teeth. This was exactly why she was glad her mother wasn't there—it's the exact conversation they would have had.

Adalynn huffed out a laugh. "You broke up with Luke and ran to Denver. You broke up with Michael and ran to Luke. I'm guessing this has something to do with Luke as well."

Rowan looked away from her sister and remained silent. The last person she wanted to talk to about this was her sister. Unfortunately, Adalynn wasn't willing to let it go.

"Hell, you even quit pageants because it got hard. The only things you never quiet were softball and dental school."

She ground her teeth together. "I didn't quit pageants because it got hard."

"Yeah…okay. You didn't place one time and you quit."

Rowan shifted toward Adalynn and glared. "I quit because after that pageant I overhead Mama tell one of the judges that she didn't know why it was so hard with me. That *you* had always been so pretty and so easy and that she just prayed I'd grow into my looks so I could start winning some of that entry money back. *That's* why I quit."

Adalynn had the grace to look shocked. "Mama wouldn't…."

She pressed her lips together and raised her eyebrows.

"But she didn't mean…."

She emphasized her look, daring Adalynn to finish her sentence.

"Is that why you became so distant?" her sister asked quietly.

She shrugged and blinked several times. "It hurt that you and Mama were so close. It always felt like I was the ugly duckling around you. It was easier not to be compared."

"I'm sorry. I didn't know. All I knew was one day my little sister didn't want anything to do with me. Why didn't you ever say anything?"

"I told Dad. A week later he took me to Little League tryouts. He told me no one was going to judge me on my hair or my smile or my sashay. All I had to do was hit, catch, and throw and those were all things I could control. I couldn't catch very well to begin with, but I was angry enough I was a really good hitter."

"I always wondered about that. Mama and Daddy had a big row about it when you came home that day."

Rowan pulled her knees up and rested her head against the back of the chair, fully facing Adalynn. "I didn't know that."

"Oh, yeah. One of the few times I remember him putting his foot down. He said you needed to do your own thing. I guess he was right."

They were quiet for several minutes. It was the first time in longer than Rowan could remember that she felt comfortable with Adalynn.

She inhaled and exhaled slowly and it was as if a huge weight was expelled with her breath.

"Luke has a relationship with Laney Faith," she said.

Adalynn's brows pinched. "The singer? What kind of relationship?"

"The kind where they swap spit."

"No way!"

"Way. I saw the pictures." The images were imprinted on her cerebral cortex.

"On the internet? I haven't seen anything and I follow all the gossip pages."

She shook her head. "Not yet. His manager brought them to the house to show me."

"Why?"

"He said because he thought I deserved to know what I was getting into. That Luke might love me but I'd never be the only woman in his life."

"That's bullshit," Adalynn said. "Luke Stone has always been a one-woman man. Even when you weren't his woman yet."

Rowan lifted her head. "What do you mean?"

"Sophomore year Linda Jo asked him to Sadie Hawkins and he turned her down because he was waiting for you to ask him."

"That hussy." She shook her head. "That was a long time ago. People change."

"Not Luke. And not when it comes to you. That boy's been stupid for you since he realized you were a girl. He wouldn't jeopardize that. Especially not after he made a public spectacle of himself."

"I want to believe that, Addy. I do, but I saw the pictures."

"Is this the same manager from before or a different one?" she asked.

"The same one."

"The one you didn't like because you thought he was a slimeball?"

"That's the one," Rowan said.

"So maybe he has a reason for showing you those pictures."

That didn't really make any sense. "Like what?"

"I don't know. To get you to leave Luke? I mean you left him before for pretty much the same reason."

"Yeah but that was…" She looked down at the worn wooden planks of the porch "…not all that different," she said softly. "The first time, I saw it happen but Brett was there. He stopped me to talk to me about my and Luke's relationship. How it wasn't good for his career and how I was holding Luke back from really taking off. I pulled away from Brett and when I turned the corner, Luke was kissing some random girl. Except…"

"Except?" Adalynn said.

"Except if someone had taken a picture of that moment, it would be almost identical to the one of him and Laney."

"How so?"

Rowan pictured the two incidents. The girl was wrapped around him, but his hands were on her hips. She focused on Adalynn. "When Luke kisses me, he wraps his arms around me so tight it's almost hard to breathe. In the picture, his hands were on her hips."

"So maybe he was trying to push her away instead of pulling her closer?"

Rowan collapsed against the chair. "Maybe."

"And maybe he was set up?" Adalynn hinted.

"But why? That doesn't make any sense." She shook her head.

"Does an asshole need a reason to pinch off pieces of shit?"

She gaped at her sister. "Does Mama know you talk like that?"

Adalynn grinned. "I'm a perfect lady in the street. Now in the—"

Rowan held up a hand. "Please don't finish that."

She winked, then grew somber. "Do you love him?"

"Yes," she said. "I've always loved him."

"Then you need to give him a chance to explain."

"Do you think he's going to give me a chance to give him a chance?"

"Stupid. For. You. Yes, he's going to give you a chance."

"What if…?"

"Don't create a problem that doesn't exist. If it turns out to be something other than a huge misunderstanding, and I don't think it is, then you can do what if."

Rowan looked at her watch. "Do you think it's too early to call?"

"One, quit trying to find excuses. Two, get your happy butt in the car and drive back to Nashville. How long of a drive was it?"

"About four and a half hours."

"Well, if you leave now, you should get there early afternoon, even if you have to stop to pee and get gas."

Rowan pushed up. "I'll go before I leave."

"I'll get you snacks for the road."

She grabbed her phone from her purse on the way and powered it up. Ten minutes later, she tossed her suitcase into the back seat of the rental.

Déjà vu set in at the number of text messages she had. Seventy-six texts in twenty-four hours—the majority of them from Luke.

She couldn't read them all and really the last couple were the most important.

Please let me know you're okay.

I'm going to make this right.

Shoot. Shoot. Shoot. What did that mean? She pressed the phone icon next to his number and raised the phone to her ear.

"You've reached Luke. Leave a message."

She groaned while she waited for the beep. "Luke, it's me. I'm sorry. I'm so sorry. I'll be there soon. Please call me back when you get this. I—" It wasn't the time to tell him she loved him. "Please."

Hoping his phone was off and he wasn't ignoring her call, she also sent a text for him to call her back.

"I got you carrot sticks and cheese," Adalynn said, coming out of the house. "Pretzels will make you thirsty. Watch your speed limit around Knoxville, the fines are horrendous."

Rowan smiled and hugged her sister tight. "Thank you."

"You'd have figured it out eventually." Adalynn pulled away and rubbed her shoulders. "I expect an invite to visit soon."

"Absolutely."

"And you should talk to Mama. She's incredibly proud of you."

"How about if I focus on one emotional crisis at a time?"

"That's probably a good idea."

Rowan climbed in the car and rolled down the window after she started the engine to say good-bye.

"Drive safe," Adalynn said.

"I will," she said.

"No really. I put some of Peepaw's peach hooch in the back."

"Adalynn!"

She threw her head back and laughed. "Call me when you get it worked out."

Rowan waved and pulled down the drive. At the first stoplight, she turned her phone back on to use the map app. She checked the speedometer and set the cruise control at five miles over the speed limit. She'd pay whatever damn ticket she got, but she had to get back to Nashville before Luke did something drastic they would both regret.

CHAPTER 30

"Luke, I don't think this is the right decision. Give me some time to find Rowan," Marla said.

Luke shook his head. He'd made up his mind. It wasn't worth it. None of it was worth if it meant losing Rowan again.

The pictures hadn't hit social media and he wasn't sure why. He'd given them to Marla and explained what had happened so she could put her PR spin on it if she had to but she hadn't had to, which unnerved him as much as having the pictures show up at the house in the first place.

"Mr. Stone?"

He approached the reception desk outside Walter Doll's office.

"I'm afraid Mr. Doll has been delayed. There's a three-car accident on the highway forty bridge exit and he was unfortunately on the bridge behind it. Do you want to reschedule?" Samantha asked.

"No. I'll wait." He turned toward the chairs in the reception area but turned around after three steps. "Actually, I'll go next door to the studio and see who's here today. Will you give me a call when he arrives?"

"Of course, but I'm really not sure how long he's going to be. Would you prefer to call him?"

He shook his head. "This is a conversation that needs to be in person."

He caught the look she shared with Marla, but he didn't care. He wasn't going to bail on the label over the phone. Although he didn't consider it bailing. If giving up music and all the shit that went with being a singer meant Rowan would be with him, he had absolutely zero fucks to give.

ROWAN FINALLY HAD to stop for gas about twenty minutes from Luke's house. It killed her to stop even five minutes, but she wasn't going to make it that far on fumes. Back in the car, she tried calling Luke again despite Adalynn's insistence to just show up. Once again it went to voice mail—not directly so she didn't think he was ignoring her. More like he had it on silent and wasn't hearing it.

She pulled out onto the access road to the highway while her phone GPS talked to her. She knew where she was for the most part, but kept the map app on to make sure she didn't take the wrong exit by mistake.

Back on the highway traffic was a little slower and heavier, but she was passing mid-town. A sea of red taillights ahead of her made her ease on the brakes and tap the steering wheel. "Come on, come on, come on."

The phone rang and her heart pitter-pattered in her chest, but a quick glanced showed it wasn't Luke calling. She answered the call and put it on speaker. "Hey, Marla."

"Oh thank god! Where are you?"

"I'm on the four-forty. What's wrong?" The urgency in Marla's voice sent her anxiety into overdrive.

"*Where* on the four-forty?"

"I'm coming up on the sixty-five exit. Why?"

"Take the exit. I'm going to send you a pin drop for Wild West Records. I need you here now."

She signaled and checked her mirror, merging to the right. "Marla, you're freaking me out. Is Luke hurt? What's *wrong*?"

"He's quitting," Marla said.

"What do you mean he's quitting? Quitting what?" Rowan looked at the phone as if it were a video call.

"He's quitting music. He showed me the pictures, Rowan. I know they look bad, but it's not what it looks like. I promise. I want to tell you why, but I'm trying to protect Laney at the same time as I keep Luke from making a huge mistake. Brett is setting them both up and I'm trying to figure out why before I expose his ass."

"I figured out something else might be going on. I just hope I'm not too late."

"Me, too. I'm hanging up so I can send you the address. Pull up to the front and valet park—I'll call down so they're expecting you. I'll try to stall as long as I can, but please try to get here quickly."

The call disconnected and a text followed a few seconds later. Under normal circumstances she'd pull over, but she didn't want to take the extra time. Keeping one eye on the road, she updated her destination. It was going to take about five extra minutes to get to downtown Nashville because of traffic.

Her impatience ramped up. Every other driver on the road had the singular purpose of getting in her way and preventing her from reaching her destination. Usually a relaxed driver, Rowan now understood why some people experienced road rage. She envisioned going full Mad Max and barreling down the road between lanes, shoving cars out of her way.

Why was Luke quitting? It didn't make sense—all he'd ever wanted to be was a country singer. For as long as she'd known him he talked about making it big in Nashville and being the next

Alan Jackson or Kenny Chesney and he was there. It didn't make any sense for him to give it all up now.

After the longest twenty-three-and-a-half minutes of her life, she pulled up to the front of Wild West Records, shoved the car in park, grabbed her phone and purse, and shot out of the car before the attendant could reach her.

"Rowan?" he asked.

She jolted to a halt. "Yes?"

"Marla said to go up to the twelfth floor, turn left out of the elevators, and follow the hall all the way to the end."

"Thank you!"

She jogged to the entrance and yanked open the door, dashing across the foyer to the elevator bank and jabbing the up button. Tapping her foot, she eyed the sign for the stairwell down the hall but there was no way she'd be able to run up twelve flights of stairs. She wasn't out of shape, but that was elite athlete level of fitness and that she was not.

Eighty-four years later, the far-left elevator opened and she repeated the whole process all over, waiting to ascend twelve floors while muttering, "Don't stop, don't stop, don't stop."

Luck was on her side and she turned sideways to slide through the doors before they opened fully. She completely ignored the framed gold and platinum records lining the hall and raced to the end. She scanned the large reception area for Marla, but the only person there was the receptionist, coming around the large desk.

"Rowan?" she asked.

"Yes," she said breathlessly.

"They just went in. Marla didn't tell me not to call Luke until I already had. He wasn't answering his phone so I called the operations manager and he said Luke was in one of the sound booths and he'd go get him. I'd literally hung up the phone when she told me not to call until you got here. Mr. Doll was in a rush and I didn't have a way to stall anymore. I'm so sorry."

"I—Okay." Rowan shook her head slightly, trying to let everything the receptionist said sink in. "Where are they? Can I interrupt?"

She smiled. "I think Marla is counting on it. This way."

Leading Rowan to a set of double wood doors, she paused. "Do you want me to knock?"

"No." Rowan turned the handle and pushed in. "Luke, stop." She stepped into the conference room, leaving the door open behind her.

She vaguely heard Marla say, "Oh thank god."

"Rowan?" Luke rose from his seat at the long table. "Rowan."

His long strides ate up the space between them. He cradled her face in his hands while his eyes searched hers, then he crushed his mouth to hers.

Wrapping her arms around his neck, she held on tight while he devoured her. She poured her heart into the kiss. If he wasn't going to give her a chance to talk, she would make him feel her love.

He ended the kiss and pressed his forehead against hers. "You're here."

Lifting his head, he said, "I'm sorry, Row. I can explain the pictures. I wasn't kissing Laney—I was trying to push her away from me. I know they looked bad, but it's the truth. I didn't want to kiss her, but I was so surprised it took me a couple of seconds to push her away and that's when the pictures were taken. I pushed her away and told her I love you. I should have told you when it happened but I was so afraid you'd leave again. I should have—"

She covered his mouth with her hand. "I love you. And I believe you."

That was all he needed for the tension to leave his body. His shoulders slumped as he dropped his forehead to hers again.

"But you can't quit music," she said. "This is your dream and you're living it."

He raised his head. "It's not. You're my dream. This is a job—

one I love, but it doesn't mean shit if you're not in my life. I won't do this without you. I don't know who took the pictures or how you got them, but if that's the kind of petty bullshit we're going to be faced with, I want nothing to do with it. I'm not going to put us in jeopardy ever again and if that means giving up music, then that's what I'll do."

"Brett gave me the pictures," she said.

His head jerked back. "What? Why?"

"I don't know." She shrugged her shoulders. "He showed up at the house with the pictures while you were here on Monday."

Luke ran a hand through his hair. "Why would he do that?"

"I can't tell you why he did it, but I can tell you why *I* did it," a soft voice said from the door.

Everyone turned to see Laney standing in the doorway, the receptionist standing next to her. Wearing yoga pants and a long shirt with her platinum hair piled on top of her head in a messy bun, she looked more sorority sister than country music's newest sweetheart.

"I'm sorry to barge in, but Marla told me what was going on and I couldn't stay out of it, as much as I want to." She focused her attention on Rowan. "I thought I had no choice. Brett has pictures of me, from when we were dating."

"You dated Brett?" Luke asked.

"For a few weeks, right after I was signed. I won't go into the gory details, but I broke it off. Except he had taken some pictures of me while I was asleep one night and he's held them over my head since. The night of the gala he said if I got you in a position where someone could take pictures of us kissing, he would delete the pictures. If not, he'd put them online." Her voice broke and tears escaped her bottom lashes. "I'm so sorry. He's been threatening me with those pictures for the past two years and I thought this was my chance to finally get rid of him for good, but he lied. No big surprise there." She huffed out a self-deprecating laugh and shook her head.

"Those are serious accusations, Laney," a deep voice said from behind them.

Rowan jumped, forgetting there was another person in the room.

"I know, Mr. Doll," Laney said.

"Do you have copies of these pictures?" he asked.

Laney shook her head. "They're on his phone though. He showed them to me again the night of the gala."

"Samantha?" Mr. Doll called.

The receptionist poked her head around the corner of the door. "Yes, Mr. Doll?"

"Is Brett in the building?" he asked.

"I'll find out," she said, disappearing from the doorway.

"Why don't we all have a seat and try to figure this out?" Mr. Doll gestured to the table.

CHAPTER 31

*L*uke walked Rowan to the table. Holding out the chair next to the one he'd sat in earlier, he took her hand in his—he wasn't going to let her go. His heart still pounded in his chest and he found himself glancing at her every other second to make sure she was really there. It was his version of pinching himself.

Walter laced his fingers together on the table. "You must be Rowan," he said.

"Yes," she said.

Luke raised their hands and kissed her knuckles.

"I'm Walter Doll. I own Wild West Records."

"I know," she said. "I researched you before Luke signed with you. You're the reason I told him he should sign."

His lips turned up under his thick, gray mustache. "I'm flattered, thank you."

"You're welcome," she said.

"All right, let's make sure I have a handle on everything while we're waiting on Brett to show up. Rowan, you were given pictures of Luke and Laney kissing at the gala?"

"Yes," she said.

"By Brett?"

"Yes. He came to Luke's house with the pictures. He insinuated that Luke had multiple relationships and that Laney was just one of many."

"I don't." His rage, at a low simmer until now, threatened to boil over. "You are the only woman in my life. The only one."

She ran her free hand over his. Realizing his grip on her fingers was too tight, he relaxed his hand.

"I believe you, Luke. And I'm sorry I doubted you. I'm sorry I let him get in my head and that I didn't stay to confront you. But seeing that *hurt*. A lot. It was college all over again and I ran. I can't promise I'm not going to get jealous of the attention women give you or get pissed off when some woman gets grabby, but I can promise I will talk to you about it."

She palmed his cheek. "I love you and I won't let you give up music for me. I may make you fire that asshole, but music is a part of you and I couldn't live with myself if you quit because of me."

"You won't have to make me do anything. He's fired. Period." There was no way in hell he could trust Brett now.

A knock at the door of the conference room drew everyone's attention. Samantha stuck her head in. "Brett is here, Mr. Doll."

"Thank you, Samantha. Send him in. And ask security to come up as well."

Samantha grinned. "Yes, sir."

Walter stood and walked around the long table, patting Luke on the shoulder as he passed. He probably wanted Luke to stay seated and to let him handle Brett, but Luke was too angry. Fuck that. He was pissed the fuck off and he'd be damned if he wouldn't confront Brett himself. He rose and stood behind Rowan's chair. She reached up and grabbed his hand.

Looking down, he gave her a reassuring smile. She squeezed his hand.

Samantha entered again and stepped to the side, letting Brett into the room. He strolled in, hands in his pockets as if he didn't have a care in the world. Hell, maybe he didn't think he had any.

"I didn't realize there was a meeting scheduled for today."

"Brett, I'm going to get right to the point," Walter said. "Did you blackmail Laney into setting up Luke so you would have pictures of them kissing to give to Rowan?"

Brett's gaze flitted between the four of them sitting at the table, pausing slightly longer on Laney and Rowan than Marla and Luke. His only tell was the almost imperceptible twitch of his eyebrow. If Luke hadn't been glaring at him so hard, he might have missed it.

"Walt, I didn't blackmail anyone. A friend of mine gave me those pictures and I felt Rowan deserved to know that Luke wasn't as faithful as he claimed to be." He shrugged. "I don't personally have a problem with it, but I know it caused them to break up before. I didn't want her to get even more involved than they are now and find out later—it could have negative consequences on his music and career."

That smug, self-righteous bastard. He'd kept looking at Laney as if to tell her to keep quiet. She had Marla next to her for support, but Luke could tell it was affecting her.

He tried to let go of Rowan's hand so he could punch that smirk off Brett's face, but she grasped his tighter.

"It's funny you bring up what happened in college," Rowan said. "Because the circumstances were almost identical, except that time you orchestrated it so I witnessed some random girl kissing Luke. This time you set it up to get pictures."

She looked up at Luke. He didn't know what she was talking about. "I'll explain later," she whispered.

Brett shook his head. "Rowan, I don't know how you remember things, but I didn't set anything up. This time or the last time."

"I remember things just fine," Laney said. "You threatened to post the pictures you have of me on the internet if I didn't get

Luke in a compromising position. You swore you'd delete them if I did what you asked, but I'd bet my next royalty check they're still on your phone."

A small bead of sweat formed at his temple and he shifted onto his heels. "I think the pressure of the spotlight is getting to you, Laney. I don't have any pictures of you on my phone."

Walter held his hand out. "Then you won't mind giving me your phone."

Brett looked at Walter's hand and really started to sweat. "Walter. You're really going to take the word of some air-headed, attention-seeking girl over me? I've been with this label for over ten years. I manage some of the biggest recording artists this label has." He gestured toward Luke.

"Not anymore you don't," Luke said.

"What?" Brett asked.

"You're fired. Whatever you have over Laney, you don't have over me. After what you put Rowan through—what you put us through—you're fired."

"We have a contract!" Brett took a step closer and Luke let go of Rowan's hand. He was going to need both of his fists when he beat the ever-living shit out of Brett.

"I've already talked to Walter. As of an hour ago, I'm no longer under contract with Wild West Records and by extension, you are no longer my manager."

"Luke," Rowan whispered.

He ran his hand over her head and through her hair. "It'll be all right."

"That's bullshit! I've worked my ass off for you, to get you where you are. You'd be nothing without me and you're going to give up your career for her?" He pointed at Rowan. "That's exactly why I tried to get rid of her. You don't have the drive necessary to succeed when she's around. You think you'd be a number-one-selling artist if you'd been together this whole time? You think you'd have the legions of adoring fans you have if you were in a relationship? No! You're where you are because women want you and guys want to be you and *I* put you there. You think you're going to have that when you're married and have kids? You think she's going to want you touring the country when you've got a house full of brats? You think she's going to give up her career for you? That bitch drags you down. You think—"

Luke was two steps away from Brett when Walter punched him in the nose. Hard.

Damn. Walter might look like someone's nice grandpa, but he had a mean jab.

Brett grabbed his face, blood gushing through his fingers. "What the fuck?"

Walter pulled a handkerchief out of his pocket and shook it out, pressing against his knuckles. "Samantha?"

Once again, she immediately popped her head around the open door. "Yes, Mr. Doll?"

"Ask security to come in and detain Mr. Carlson while his office is searched. Have IT go through his computer as well. Once Mr. Carlson turns over his phone for search, he'll be free to collect his personal belongings from his office and be escorted out of the building."

She didn't even try to hide her smile. "On it."

Security must have been right outside the door because they entered a few seconds later. One man pulled a chair away from the conference table and wheeled it over to Brett while the other officer pushed him down into it.

"Now, Brett, your phone. You can either give it to me—unlocked—or I can have these nice gentlemen retrieve it for me."

Brett glanced up at the two men on either side of him. They both looked like they wanted him to choose the second option. He shifted and dug it out of his pocket, holding his thumb on it before handing it to the security guard on his right.

Walter took it and promptly handed it to Laney. "I'll let you take care of that."

Laney's fingers flitted over the screen while Marla looked over her shoulder. Luke knew the exact moment Marla saw the pictures. Her lips pinched and she took the phone from Laney. "You need to make sure they're not on his cloud as well."

A few minutes later, she slid the phone across the table to Walter. "I think I got them all. Laney wasn't the only one."

He picked up the phone and held it out to Brett, who was still holding his nose. "If I catch wind that you have more pictures—of anyone—and any of them make their way onto the internet, I will make sure you are prosecuted to the fullest extent possible." He looked at the security guards. "Please escort Mr. Carlson to his office, then out of the building."

The two men each grabbed Brett's upper arms and led him out.

A thick, heavy silence filled the room upon his departure.

"Laney, I'm very sorry you experienced that and, more importantly, that you didn't feel you could come talk to me about it."

Laney swallowed hard and nodded.

"I want to make sure you have whatever you need to get through this, so get with Marla and your manager and let me know. The label will do whatever it takes to make this right. *I* will do whatever it takes to make this right."

"Thank you," she whispered. She rose from her chair and walked across the room. At the door, she paused and turned, looking at Rowan. "I really am sorry. For what it's worth, he pushed me away almost immediately and told me he loved you. That you were the only woman he'd ever been in love with and he wouldn't do anything to jeopardize your relationship."

"Thank you," Rowan said.

Laney nodded and walked out.

"Now," Walter said, walking back to the head of the table. "Luke, you have some decisions to make."

Luke sat next to Rowan and took her hand again. "What do you want me to do?"

"I want you to live your dream. I want you to make music," she said.

"As long as you're with me." He wouldn't do it without her.

"I'm not going to go anywhere this time," she said.

He pressed his lips against hers, sealing her promise. She opened under his mouth while her hand stole behind his neck, holding him tightly. He would never get enough of kissing her.

A deep throat clearing broke them apart. A blush stole across her cheeks and he winked. They had plenty of time to catch up on that later.

"All right," Walter said, clearing his throat again. "We'll need to find you a new manager, but if you're still good with the terms of the contract we drew up on Monday we can go ahead and sign it."

"I want Marla," he said.

"What?" Her head jerked. "I'm not a manager."

"You do everything a manager does," Luke said. "You take better care of me and my career than anyone else ever has."

"I—I don't know what to say."

"Say yes," Rowan said.

"Yes. Yes!" She laughed. "I would love to be your manager, Luke. Thank you. I won't let you down."

"I know," he said. "Walter, I don't have any issues with the contract, but I have a more pressing appointment right now. How does a week from next Wednesday sound?"

"What do you need to do?" Rowan asked. "We're here, you should just sign the contract now."

He gazed into her earnest eyes. "I need to marry you. So right now, we're going to the courthouse for a license and we're going to get married by the Justice of the Peace. Then we're going to call your parents and my mom and we'll drive to Johnson City or Flat Holler or wherever they want to put the church wedding together and we'll get married again."

"Oh, really?" she asked.

"Yes," he said. "Really."

"There's just one problem with your plan," she said.

He sucked in a deep breath. He'd shoot down any argument she had. He wasn't going to go another day without her being legally his woman. "What's that?"

"I need to return my rental car," she said.

He smirked. "I have a manager that can take care of that for us."

CHAPTER 32

*O*ne *Year Later*

Rowan gritted her teeth and plastered a smile on her face as the contraction spasmed through her.

Today of all days. She'd been sure the spasms she'd had through the day had been more Braxton Hicks since she'd been having them for the past week or so, but this was the real deal.

Sweat broke out on her forehead as she counted through the contraction and tried to breathe through her nose. As the pain ebbed, she checked her watch. The contractions were still eighteen minutes apart. Doing a quick calculation in her head, she might have enough time for the Single of the Year category winner to be announced before she really had to panic and let Luke know she was in labor.

She looked down at her belly. "You are going to be as big a pain in the ass as your daddy," she whispered. She couldn't even be excited about the fact that they were two rows behind Keith Urban and Nicole Kidman. Nicole had looked at Rowan's belly earlier and smiled at her. She smiled at her!

Luke finished his conversation with whoever he was talking to several rows back and returned to their seats as the chimes indicated the commercial break was over and the awards show would be going live again.

He kissed her cheek as he sat down and rubbed her belly. "Sorry. That was the songwriter Marla has been trying to set me up with for the last three months."

"It's okay," she said.

He leaned back and stared at her hard. "Are you okay?"

She smiled and nodded. "Yes. Just uncomfortable. I'm ready for this baby to be out." Whoo boy, was she ever.

He stood and held her upper arm. "Why didn't you say something? Let's go. We're not staying if you're not comfortable."

She slapped his hand away. "Sit down. I'm going to be uncomfortable no matter where we are so we might as well be here where you're up for two awards."

He eased into his plush theater seat. "Row, I'm not kidding. If you'd rather be home with your feet in my lap while I rub them, we'll leave. I'll message the driver to come around and get us."

"I'm sure." She pointed at the stage. "Watch the show."

LUKE STOLE another glance at Rowan. He didn't believe she was all right. She'd been having false contractions for the last few days and she had that same look on her face. Plus, she kept glancing at her watch.

His first category was up next and, win or lose, they were going home after that. The Academy of Country Music Awards was nowhere near as important as Rowan and their baby. She needed to be at home, with her feet up.

The announcer introduced the presenters who walked on stage and Rowan squeezed his hand as they announced the best song category. It felt like coming full circle. He'd recorded the song he'd sung at Rowan's almost wedding and it had gone platinum. Everyone thought he was a shoo-in to win this year, but he had some stiff competition. He just loved the fact he was nominated for the song that started it all.

They called his name and panned to him in the audience. He waved at the camera focused on him as Rowan's grip strengthened. Looking at her, he knew immediately she was not all right.

"What is it?" he asked.

"My water broke," she whispered.

He leapt to his feet. "What?"

She squeezed her eyes closed and clenched her teeth, crushing the bones of his hand. Holy shit, she was in labor.

He looked around and waved to get an usher's attention. The guy looked at the stage and back at Luke, seemingly confused that Luke was trying to get him over.

Luke vaguely heard his name being called again and suddenly people began slapping him on the back and hugging him. That was great and all, but the baby hadn't been born yet. The usher was trying to push through the well-wishers and Luke reached through the crowd to grab his jacket sleeve.

"Sir, you need—"

"To go to the hospital, get the paramedics here now. My wife is in labor."

The guy looked down at Rowan, blanched, and ran up the aisle.

"Luke. Luke!" Marla pushed through. "You won. You need to go accept your award."

"What?" He looked around and realized everyone was looking at him expectantly. "Marla, Rowan's in labor. I need an ambulance. Go—" He gestured toward the stage. "I don't know, but I need to get her out of here."

"Luke, go accept your award." Rowan's grip had eased. The contraction had passed but she was drenched in sweat and her face was flushed.

"You are out of your mind." He scooped her up and side-stepped out of the aisle as people made room for him. Heading toward the exit, he heard Marla's voice fill the room.

"Ladies and gentlemen, as you may have noticed, Luke and Rowan have a pressing matter to attend to. He thanks everyone who made this possible and will have a more prepared announcement later."

Applause and whistles followed him out of the auditorium. The paramedics met them in the lobby and transferred Rowan to a gurney, which they pushed out to the waiting ambulance.

Seventeen minutes after reaching the hospital Rowan gave birth to a very tiny, very angry little girl. Less than an hour later, she stared at him groggily while their baby girl rested on her chest.

"You won," she whispered.

He laid his hand on their daughter's back and felt her tiny body rise and fall with her breaths. Brushing Rowan's hair back from her face, he kissed her forehead. "I know."

ACKNOWLEDGMENTS

Writing never happens in a vacuum and this book is no different.

Thank you to Geri for helping me plot out the idea for this duet at RWA in Denver in 2018.

Kelley, for helping me work through some plot points.

Give Me Books Promotions and all the fabulous reviewers and bloggers who help spread the word.

Jessica, as ALWAYS, for your fabulous editing.

Anna, Melissa, Josie, Taryn, Taylor, and Freya — you ladies ROCK.

My family, for your continuing belief and encouragement.

And always, ALWAYS, you—the reader. Without you this is just another story I made up in my head.

ABOUT THE AUTHOR

Tarina is an award winning author who has spent her entire life in and around the military - first as a dependent and then as an enlisted Air Force member. She uses her life as inspiration for many of her stories, because truth is stranger (and funnier) than fiction.

Tarina is still active duty and a single mom of six-year-old twins. Her favorite hobby is sleep. She has delusions of retiring from the military and being a stay-at-home mom.

Stay Connected
Website
Email
Newsletter

ALSO BY TARINA DEATON

The Combat Hearts Series

Stitched Up Heart

Half-Broke Heart

Locked-Down Heart

Rescued Heart

Imperfect Heart

Holiday Heart (only available to newsletter subscribers)

The Jilted Duet

Make Me Believe

Believe In Me (coming Fall 2019)

Susan Stoker World Novel (coming July 2019)

www.ingramcontent.com/pod-product-compliance
Lightning Source LLC
Chambersburg PA
CBHW061433210726
48287CB00007B/2199